THE BLACK FREIGHTER

ALSO BY FRED G. BAKER

FICTION

The Black Freighter

ZONA: The Forbidden Land

The Detective Sanchez/Father Montero Mysteries:
An Imperfect Crime
Desert Sanctuary

The Modern Pirate Series:
Seizing the Tiger
Prowling Tiger
Restless Tiger
Raging Tiger

NON-FICTION

Growing Up Wisconsin:

The Life and Times of Con James Baker

The Ancestors of Con James Baker of
Des Moines, Iowa, and Chicago, Illinois,
Volumes 1–3

The Descendants of John Baker (ca. 1640–1704) of Hartford,
Connecticut, Through Thirteen Generations,
Volumes 1–2

Light from a Thousand Campfires,
with Hannah Pavlik

The Black Freighter

A Caribbean Spy Thriller

Fred G. Baker

Other Voices Press
Golden, Colorado

Published by Other Voices Press, Golden, Colorado

ISBN 978-1-949336-14-6

Cover Design by Nick Zelinger, NZ Graphics.com
Southwest Clip Art by GoGraph.com
All Rights Reserved by Fred G. Baker.

Printed in the United States.

Acknowledgments

I would like to thank the following people for their aid and support in the writing and production of this book, Dr. Hannah Pavlik, for her support and encouragement; my beta readers who provided helpful comments and ideas; Donna Zimmerman for word processing; and Nick Zelinger for cover design.

Chapter 1

Tuesday, March 6

Grenada, West Indies

The passengers were already fed up with the wait to get through security screening at the Maurice Bishop International Airport. The screening was tighter than usual because of the recent demonstrations in Saint George's, the capital city of the small island nation of Grenada. Threats of violence were taken seriously during a sensitive period like this when a contentious national election divided Grenadians against one another. Rumors of outside interference in the election filled the air.

Robert Wilson stood inside a kiosk at the airport terminal, watching passengers deal with the chaos of modern travel. They jostled each other, tempers flaring occasionally, as they made their way through the screening line.

He was glad he wasn't traveling today. He was just killing time as he waited for a certain Caribbean Airlines flight to arrive from Caracas. He wasn't meeting anyone from the flight, but he was interested in who might be on board.

As he paged through a tourist pamphlet, he noticed that one of the many terminal televisions was carrying a story about the recent volcanic eruption on Grenada. The video shown on the TV was taken years before on the island of Montserrat, where the Soufrière Hills volcano exploded. It served to show what might happen if the current eruption went completely out of control. It was dramatic enough to cause tourists to stop in their tracks and stare in awe before hurrying to their departure gates.

The rush to evacuate tourists from the island had accelerated when the Grenada government raised the volcano alert level from yellow to orange and noted that it might go red shortly. An undersea volcano called Kick 'em Jenny had recently begun venting gases and pouring lava onto the seafloor. It was an ancient volcano that hadn't erupted since the 1930s, but it did occasionally belch steam and sulfur dioxide into the sea, poisoning the water and threatening maritime traffic.

The government had issued a five-mile exclusion zone around the volcano because the gases could build up in the water and change its density. That meant that a ship sailing through the gassy water might not be as buoyant as usual. Ships could actually sink in the bubbly sea.

In any case, most tourists had not included a volcanic eruption in their vacation plans. The American government and some other countries had issued an advisory, and a few touring companies had rerouted their cruise ships. Many tourists had decided to vacate the island. The problem was that there were only so many flights to and from the island every day, so all airline seats had booked up quickly. Nobody was really in panic mode yet, but a red alert would send foreigners into hysteria.

Wilson checked his watch, then purchased a cup of coffee at the café and loitered outside the airport exit. He positioned himself where he could remain unobserved as he watched passengers depart the Caracas flight. He checked the faces of all the men who exited the baggage area. He took their photos on his cell phone surreptitiously. He was surprised that none of the men from the flight were the ones listed in his briefing file. *That was odd. Who were these men?*

He walked to his rental car and watched as a few more people exited the terminal. He rubbed his hands over his face to ward off fatigue. He must focus on the work ahead. It was important, possibly dangerous, work. And he had only a week to do it.

Chapter 2

Tuesday

Driving from the airport back to his hotel on Grand Anse Main Road, Wilson had time to think about the challenge that lay ahead. He had come to Grenada on assignment, posing as a journalist covering the upcoming national election. He was collecting information about what was really happening behind the surface of the election campaigns. He was an analyst and was to report back to headquarters what he discovered. It sounded easy enough, but there were strong political undercurrents, some of them foreign, most of them clandestine.

There were reports of political intrigue before the national election, and a few sources suggested that the current government—one friendly to America—might fall. In an open and fair election, that would be considered democracy in action. But the rumors suggested that outside influence was at play, and that would be a problem.

Wilson pulled the Toyota Noah minivan up to the guard station of the Hempstead Resort. The guard came out of his little shack with a clipboard, checked Wilson's ID, and noted the license number of the vehicle, R344, a Hertz rental.

"Good night, Mr. Wilson. How you be?" The guard named Leslie was a huge black man with a friendly smile who prided himself on knowing the names of all the guests within two days of arrival.

"Hello, Leslie. Doin' fine today." Wilson had not yet gotten used to the local tradition that anything after noon was considered evening and any time after dark required you to wish passersby "Good night," even if you were just arriving.

Wilson drove to the small car park and switched off the engine. He had started parking in the inner area due to recent shenanigans by protesters at the public park nearby. A few men had been seen within the Hempstead compound, men who should not be there.

He walked to his room on the second floor of the main building where he had an ocean view, Grand Anse Beach only fifty feet away. He walked immediately to the front window, opened the sliding glass door, and stepped out onto the balcony. He picked up the binoculars from the small plastic table and raised them to his eyes.

Yes, the long black ship was still at anchor nearly a half mile offshore. It was a freighter of some sort with two cranes mounted on its deck and several visible containers. The lettering COBRA was painted in white on the side of its hull, and it had an identification number and name on the stern: the *Shanghai Maiden*. He had managed to sail past the ship three days before on a rented sailboat, giving it a once-over. He had memorized the name and number. He had seen several Chinese seamen on board.

He had sent an email back to his control at Langley asking for more information about the ship. It had arrived in port three weeks ago and had never moved from its present anchorage. That was odd for a cargo ship that had to load and unload in order to maintain its shipping schedule and turn a profit.

The ship had two masts on it, one on the forecastle and one aft. They didn't have spars on them, so they probably were not in current use for sailing. The ship had a satellite dish, a radar dish, and several antennas, some of which were attached to the masts. This number was not normally found on a freighter.

Wilson called the mystery ship the *Black Freighter*.

Wilson walked into the bathroom and washed his face after a long and warm tropical day. He looked in the mirror at his suntanned features, where worry showed in lines around his brown eyes. He was tired from a few late nights and the days of conversations with locals and government officials about the upcoming election. He combed his gray-tinted brown hair, noting the sunburn on his somewhat crooked nose, a reminder of his college boxing days.

He checked his voice mail and email before leaving the room, then he walked along the darkening pathway toward the hotel's beach bar. Tiny frogs sang out in high-pitched chirps from their hiding places in the lush vegetation that lined the path and filled the landscaped spaces between buildings. He crossed the inner courtyard and made his way to the main swimming pool, where several hotel guests were still entertaining themselves. Palm trees, red bougainvillea, ginger, and other plants made the grounds feel like natural jungle in a parklike environment. The smell of ripe mango fruit filled the air. The sound of reggae music drifted toward him as he made his way to the center of activity.

He entered the beach bar, which opened right onto the beach and the swimming pool. It had a straight mahogany bar on one side and was open to the beach at the front, with the pool to the right. A dozen tables stood inside the café, with high-tops just outside the canopy. The serving staff of three was challenged when the place neared capacity on weekends. Wilson had learned that going directly to the bar was the best strategy if he wanted a drink within fifteen minutes of arrival.

"Rum and ginger ale, Gordon," he called cheerily to the bartender, a very tall man who wore a black bow tie, a white shirt, and a broad smile every evening he worked. His well-groomed

Afro and goatee, along with the square-framed glasses he wore, gave him the air of a young jazz musician or a university professor.

"Comin' right up, Mr. Wilson. How ya tonight?"

"Doin' good," Wilson replied. "And you, keeping out of trouble?"

"Tryin', you know. It difficult with the election coming up. People come and argue for NSP and the blue. Others come in to drink and want the GPC and orange to win. I'm just a bartender. I gotta agree wid both sides, so I just listen, listen, and listen."

Wilson and Gordon bumped fists. Wilson laughed as Gordon handed him a rum and ginger ale, a much better drink than a rum and Coke. The ginger brought out the flavor of the rum; the Coke killed it.

"So who's going to win? I hear all sorts of things that the GPC will win and there will be a sea of orange T-shirts all over. Then I talk to someone wearing blue and they say the NSP will win," Wilson said, slapping his palm flat on the bar. "They're both sure they will win."

The NSP, or National Standard Party, with its blue jerseys and placards, was currently in power and had run a moderate and stable government for more than twenty years. The GPC, or Grenada People's Congress, the orange party, had been the opposition party for two decades, running in all the elections as a populist and social reform party. They didn't win many elections, but they always put up a spirited game.

Gordon leaned forward and lowered his voice. "The smart money say that NSP never lost an election and they incumbent. So they hard to beat."

"But some people say the GPC has lots of money to spend this time around. That's why they have so many TV ads and banners everywhere."

Just then they were joined by Oliver Morant, the bar manager for the Hempstead, an older man who had been through the island's political seasons many times. He said, "That the big question. Where does Hjarad Senjai get de money for all dem political ads, do you suppose?"

"Outside money?" asked Gordon. He knew that most NSP supporters were convinced that foreign cash was behind the GPC. It never failed to get a rise out of Oliver Morant.

Morant was a big man with graying hair and a marked stoop. He walked over to the bar and stood next to Gordon. "The opposition certainly got more money to spend in this election than ever they had in the past." He lowered his voice and brought his dark features close to Wilson's face. He whispered, "Some say it's Chinese money."

Gordon picked up the thought. "But nobody knows where that money is coming from. Nuh? Who got money for dat?"

"And not only who, but why?" Morant whispered.

Wilson had heard this before. The GPC had lost the last three elections because they had put up marginal candidates and couldn't raise money. In fact, the man they were now putting forward as their party leader and their candidate for prime minister was Hjarad Senjai, the same man who had lost the last three elections. He was not a likeable man, and many people said they would not accept him as PM if he was elected. And yet again, the GPC had put him up as their candidate, along with many others who had run and lost previous elections. It just seemed that the GPC had no clue how to win office.

"And the GPC promising too many things, promising every child goin' to have a computer for school, everyone goin' to get a job, everyone goin' to get free health care, everyone goin' to get basic income. How they goin' to do dat?" Gordon paused. "Wid no money?"

"But this year Senjai seems flush with cash. He's on TV a lot and gives speeches all over the country," Wilson said. The GPC had a huge war chest this election. This concerned Wilson. *What was different this time?*

"I think it's Chinese money." Morant lowered his voice again. "He mighty friendly with the Chinese companies that do business here on the island. He was minister of public works, you know. He gave that big Chinese company its first construction job three years ago—the national stadium contract. He been friends with dem ever since."

The television over the bar suddenly flashed an orange banner on the screen, and a campaign ad for the opposition party ran loudly, with the PM candidate, Senjai, shouting out promises. He would make every man on the island prosperous with government programs, but he did not say how he would pay for it all. Then he talked about how the Chinese government stood ready to invest capital in industry on the island.

A peculiarity of the GBTV—Grenada Broadcasting, the only television station on the island—was that they ran a network disclaimer after every single political ad on the air. Lately there were so many orange ads appearing back-to-back with the disclaimer that it was rather monotonous.

"How you gonna pay fo' dat?" a man at the bar shouted and then he and a friend laughed. "Give it to me!" he yelled. "I got no money to pay now. Why not give me some dat money?" Several customers laughed along with them.

It seemed that many Grenadians had a better understanding of how money worked than the candidate for the opposition,

Senjai. But politicians never failed to make promises they would never keep, even if they were elected.

Gordon moved down the bar to serve another guest. Morant looked around the room to see if any other customers needed help. He returned to the conversation. "Senjai made three trips to China since then—all paid for by Wong Construction Company. Since then they won three more contracts from the Grenada government."

"You think they gave him something? Money?" Wilson asked. He had heard rumors about Senjai receiving money before, but they seemed to be just that—rumors. "Maybe money for his campaign? That happens in the US all the time."

"I don't know," Morant said. "But he drivin' a big Mercedes car now. *Brand new.* That's expensive with the government import tax. Where he get that kind of money? It ain't from his government salary."

Gordon came back. "An' the news poll showing orange side, the GPC, very high, right up with the blue side. But I don't know anyone who wants to vote for orange. How can that be?"

Wilson smiled at Gordon's enthusiasm. He had learned that Gordon was the man to know for information about what was really going on in this country. He seemed to have a knack for gossip and for getting people to talk.

Two large groups of customers entered the bar and looked around for tables. As he rushed off to seat them, Morant said, "Where dat girl Simone? She late again?"

Wilson turned around on his barstool and watched the place fill up with dinner guests. A group of Venezuelan men came in. They were attending the economic forum at the hotel conference center a short distance away. They were a rowdy crowd and demanded rum punch cocktails immediately as they sat down at a table by the pool. Wilson wondered what kind of economic conference they could possibly have, given their currently failing economy at home.

Suddenly there was an altercation at the far end of the bar where one of the Venezuelans demanded a drink. He had apparently pushed one of the locals out of his way, and harsh words were exchanged. A mix of Spanish swearing, punctuated by Grenadian insults, led Morant to intervene bodily in the argument. The bar manager, who had been a professional wrestler at one time, simply clamped the angry Latin in a bear hug, pinning the man's arms to his sides, and carried him out of the bar to the beach.

"Stay here till you can be friendly. We all friendly here." Morant then marched away, leaving the man to fume on his own for a while.

A warm breeze filled the bar as a light rain began falling, creating a pattering sound on the metal roof of the establishment. Rhythmic island music, a ska tune now, drifted over the clientele of the beach bar.

Wilson saw a large cruise ship lumber into the main port of Saint George's four miles away, all its lights glaring against the water. It seemed as though every cabin and deck light was illuminated for the show. Wilson wondered if all cruise lines would stop docking at Grenada now that the volcano was acting up. The volcano. It was a new factor that had everybody on edge. People were already nervous about the upcoming election.

Just then a banner flashed across the TV screen: *Breaking News*. Gordon called for the people in the bar to be quiet and then turned up the volume on the television.

A very calm woman appeared on-screen. "We have just received news that Neville Charles, who is the National Standard

Party's candidate for minister from West Saint George's, has been seriously injured in a fight at a campaign rally. Mr. Charles was speaking at an event near the city market where a large crowd of his supporters had gathered earlier this evening. It seems that several rowdy and possibly drunk men dressed in orange shirts typical of the Grenada People's Congress crashed the event. They began chanting campaign slogans for the opposition. A lot of shovin' and name-callin' erupted, and soon the GPC supporters shouted down the candidate. Several men ran onto the stage and snatched the microphone from Mr. Charles's hand. Then a fight broke out between the newcomers and Charles's supporters. Some of the men had cricket bats, which came into play, and a general riot resulted. Mr. Charles and several other NSP members were injured and removed to hospital. Police arrested nearly two dozen men . . . More news later."

There were many comments from the customers as they digested this news, which created a sense of fear and uncertainty. Everyone seemed upset.

A Grenadian man said, "This is bad."

A woman said, "This isn't right, this violence."

One of the Venezuelans commented in Spanish, "*¿Amigos, es como neustras ciudad, no?*" This was just like home. He led his comrades in jovial discussion. They all laughed raucously. Some of the Grenadians stared at the men, muttering their distain. The Venezuelans curtailed their mirth.

Gordon looked at Wilson with concern. "Mr. Wilson, this is not like our Grenada. We argue but then have peaceful elections. None of this fighting."

"What has changed?" Wilson asked, curious.

"It's those outsiders," said Morant. "The Chinese. The Venezuelans. Who knows? But this is not like us. This is like it was when the damn Cubans were here—always meddling."

Wilson tossed down the last of his rum and ginger and stood up from the bar. "Well, I have an early morning. I'll see you gentlemen tomorrow." He nodded to Gordon and Morant and to the others at the bar who noticed his departure.

He sauntered back toward his room quietly, slipping through the vegetation-lined paths as he smoked a small cigar and enjoyed the singing of the frogs. But he did not return to his room. Instead, he followed the path that led to the side of the property where there was a gap in the fence used by the lawn maintenance staff. It led to a side street, not much more than a sandy lane that ran from the beach to the rear of the hotel where the trash dumpsters were stored. He headed for the beach, with light provided by the half moon in a cloud-cluttered sky guiding his way.

***

He walked directly to the path that followed the beach and wandered past several other resorts and beach properties. He took his time, puffing on his cigar as he shuffled through the loose sand on this warm tropical evening. As he walked along, he greeted the night watchmen who stood silently in their cotton uniforms in the dark at the more exclusive resorts.

Soon he heard the sounds of the establishment he was seeking. It was the small rum shop and bar called Mingo's that was located on the beach, away from the tourist trade. It wasn't much more than a shack with a tin roof over a simple structure of posts and wooden siding. The floor was sand, and the bar was a long counter propped up on barrels with a plain set of shelves for a backbar. The rum drinks flowed easily and cheaply. Spirits were high.

It was where fishermen and entrepreneurs of a sort mingled after hours for sport and for profit. Soca music, that favorite style of Grenada, filled the air, and a few couples danced next to the bar.

Wilson sought out one man in the mixed crowd, a man who would normally seem a bit out of place here. He was sitting at a tall table at the back talking to a lean, dark woman. Wilson would not have taken him for an English lord based on his current costume of worn khakis and a battered straw hat—maybe a beachcomber or fisherman hoping to attract a tourist to his boat for a day of sport fishing—not the British adjunct consul, Sir Darius Lightchurch, stationed in Grenada on assignment. He had a neatly trimmed beard, and thinning hair framed his reddish complexion, the result of years at sea. He looked like an English professor or even like that British actor who played in *Jurassic Park*. At least that's who came to mind when Wilson first met him. He was an affable man with a good store of off-color jokes that came out after a few glasses of scotch, his favorite libation.

"Robert, you were able to make it. How clever." He spoke in a quiet Oxford style, perhaps slurring his words a little from an evening of scotch sampling, as he kept his head low, disguising his features. "This young lady is Madeline Caron, an old friend of mine and someone who is quite discreet."

"Good evening, Darius. You seem to be having a pleasant time." Wilson looked at the stunning Madeline and noted her tight-fitting wrap. Her black hair was braided in a crown on top of her head, setting off her caramel-colored skin and light-brown eyes. "Good evening, Madeline. How are you?"

"Fine, Mr. Wilson." She smiled and slipped from the stool she had occupied. "I'll get us fresh drinks, if you'll be drinkin' the same as his lordship here." As she turned, Wilson noticed the slight bulge of her dress at the small of her back that suggested she did not travel unprepared.

Lord Lightchurch followed his gaze. "She is pleasant to look at and also serves as my security team." He finished the last of his drink and set the glass on the table. He chuckled. "Cutbacks, old boy. I used to rank at least two security men. Now I have Madeline. Much more pleasant spending time with her than the stiff silent types. The dark Ray-Bans always made me nervous."

"We can speak in front of her?"

"Oh yes. She has full clearance and is very helpful with information gathering." The old gentleman snickered. "I think most people assume she's some sort of escort, so they speak freely around her. They'd probably tell her their deepest secrets if I wasn't nearby."

"I heard that, old man." Madeline returned with two generous pours of Glenlivet and a gin and tonic for herself. She smiled at Lightchurch. "You're really like my grandfather sometimes."

"Ouch, that hurt. So it's grandfather now; yesterday I was your kindly old man." Lightchurch and Madeline chuckled at the old joke.

Wilson observed the two carefully and decided that he could share his information with them both tonight. After a moment Wilson said, "Let's compare notes. Do you have anymore info about the containers?"

Lightchurch leaned in to whisper his reply. "Yes and no." He paused as he formulated his response. "We know the containers were brought in two months ago—sixteen of them. But there may have been more since then. They come in under the aegis of

Wong Construction Company, but they have never been opened since arrival."

"And the other containers—how many?"

"We don't know exactly. They arrive in small batches with other equipment and containers that are opened and used right away." Lightchurch sipped his scotch. "Customs has them all listed as material for the commercial building they're working near Quarantine Point. You know—that huge iron monstrosity that will overlook the bay. It's supposedly a hotel of some sort, but it seems too big for that. Lots of steel compared to anything else on this island."

"Yes, I drove by the site a few days ago. It's extensive." Wilson swirled his whiskey in the glass before drinking. "They have a lot of security in place there, fencing and guard patrols. Seems excessive for a construction site."

"And they have a lay-down area with many containers arranged along the back of the site where no one can see them being opened." Lightchurch stopped and raised his hands in the air, palms up. "What the hell are they doing?"

"I'd like to get in there and take a look inside one of those containers," Wilson said. "Did you get the list of the ones we know about?"

"Yes." Lightchurch nodded to Madeline, who subtly passed a slip of paper to Wilson as she shifted her arm next to his. "This is what we can tell. These numbers are for the containers we suspect so far. There may be others."

"I'm going for a walk out that way in the morning. I'll try to get an angle and read off some of the numbers on the containers in the back."

"How will you get close?"

"Oh, didn't I tell you? I'm a bird-watcher sometimes."

Lightchurch laughed. "It might work. Just don't let them see you."

"And what news about the Russians working at the airport?" Wilson changed the subject.

"They have a legitimate contract to upgrade the radar and communications systems at Maurice Bishop. But I still suspect them of some sort of espionage. It's in their blood, and I wouldn't doubt they're up to something."

"When do they finish the work?"

"According to my sources, they'll finish at the end of the month, just after the election." Lightchurch grimaced. "It's interesting timing, isn't it?"

Wilson signaled the barman for another round of drinks and thought quietly for a few moments. "And I suppose the last thing is the black freighter. Any news?"

"Nothing new there. The ship was originally registered in Hong Kong but has been steaming overseas for years. It never comes into a British port and was reregistered in Macao three years ago."

The drinks arrived, and they toasted to good fortune. Wilson looked puzzled. "Ironic that it was of Hong Kong registry but now works Caribbean waters."

"Suspicious is what you mean," Madeline chimed in, her eyes flashing as she spoke.

Wilson looked around to ensure that no one was within earshot. "We've learned a few things about the *Shanghai Maiden*. She's spent much of her time off the coast of China, either running to North Korea or between Chinese ports with a variety of cargo, as far as our source could tell. He deals mostly with trade in the South China Sea." Wilson watched Lightchurch for his reaction.

"It's consistent with your observations of the freighter just lying about," Lightchurch commented. "Curiouser and curiouser." He raised his eyebrows.

"We need some answers," Wilson said as he finished his single malt. "Thanks for the drinks. I have an early morning or I'd stay longer. I want to take a hike up to Quarantine Point. See what I can see." He threw some money on the table and stood up to leave.

"Let me know what you find on your bird-watching trip." Lightchurch chuckled and raised his scotch. Then he leaned forward and whispered, "Be careful, Robert. The whole political climate here reminds me of other unsettling places I've been posted to before trouble began. Jakarta, Tehran, Cairo . . . I feel that mischief and revolution are in the air."

Chapter 3

Wednesday

The next morning, Wilson woke early and had breakfast at the hotel as usual, reading a local birding guidebook and asking his waiter a few causal questions about local wildlife. He finished breakfast by 8:00 a.m. and left the hotel on foot, wearing khaki pants, a blue cotton button-up shirt, and a Miami Marlins baseball cap. He traveled along the beach to the public park and then turned onto the lane that led to the small shopping center nearby. That in turn led to the Morne Rouge Road, the two-lane blacktop highway that climbed along the coast to Quarantine Point and continued west to Morne Rouge Bay. That was the next embayment along the coast west of Grand Anse. It was a beautiful deep bay with a pocket beach and a resort of the same name. The road led right past the Wong Construction site where the mysterious containers were stored.

It was a pleasant morning, and a light breeze blew in from the sea. The sky was clear but offered a few clouds that could carry rain later in the day. Traffic along the road was light as usual, and no one seemed interested in a tourist who was obviously involved in the sport of bird identification.

There was one exception to this observation; the Chinese guard at the gate of the construction site eyed Wilson as if he were a saboteur and watched him as he proceeded up the road. The road continued up the hill to a ridge that reached up to the coast range on the left and that ran out to Quarantine Point on the right. The point took its name from the olden days when any newcomers from ships with a chance of plague or other illnesses were harbored until the local medical staff cleared them of disease. Now it was a hilltop park with a full view of Grand Anse to the northeast and Morne Rouge Bay to the southwest.

Wilson turned left and scurried up a gravel road that led to the ridge behind the Wong site. The lane ended at a cluster of new houses at the tree line, where a small trail ran off into dry forest. It was an ideal location for bird-watching and for an approach to the rear of the Wong property for an overview of their operations.

He followed the trail through the brush for a quarter mile, then deviated from its path and cut downward between small mango and other wild fruit trees toward the Wong Construction site. He reached a point where the vegetation was very dense but where he could gain a view of the rear of the construction site, its south side, below him. He noted that cyclone fencing, or the Chinese equivalent of it, encircled the entire property.

The contractors had cleared the front of the property and had knocked down many trees near its rear boundary as well. The main building for the commercial center, on its north side toward the sea and main road, was still just a forest of girders for the proposed hotel near the front, but large warehouse structures had been completed behind that on the east and the south. A broad assortment of machinery and sea containers were arrayed in the center of the site where work was under way. Several of those containers were open, and Wilson could see stacks of pipes, fittings, lumber, and other objects inside the open doors. A lay-down area of girders, steel sheeting, concrete blocks, and other building materials were arranged neatly to the west side of the lot.

The construction site was a hive of activity as heavy machinery, including bulldozers and a tracked excavator, dug out foundations in an open area up front while cranes lifted iron girders onto concrete pads nearby. It looked like four different buildings were under way at the front of the site. Men and vehicles scurried here and there, moving supplies and tools where they were needed. Three large warehouse-like structures were already built near the west and south boundaries, possibly for maintenance or other facilities.

Forty or fifty additional sea containers formed a dense array at the back of the property, apparently hidden there. These did not appear to be currently in use because their doors were closed, and Wilson could make out padlocks sealing many of them at the top and bottom of each door. These containers interested him, so he began making a list of the identification numbers on the steel doors. There were two sets of numbers, one that seemed to match the standard ID system—four letters followed by seven digits—and then a set of larger numbers that may have been some sort of Wong Construction internal code. This took nearly an hour using a pen to crib the numbers onto a small notebook he had with him. He could not see all the numbers clearly due to the rising haze of the morning air and some stray tree branches.

When he finished writing down the numbers of the locked containers, he began noting the IDs of the open containers in the active construction area. He could not see all these numbers because machinery and stacks of lumber blocked his view. He would compare the numbers of all the containers to the list he had received from Lightchurch when he returned to his hotel.

Wilson had just put the notebook in his shirt pocket when two Chinese men in uniform suddenly appeared in the forest just below his location. He immediately crouched down behind a low hibiscus bush and kept still. The men were dressed in brown uniforms similar to those worn by mall cops everywhere in the world, many of the uniforms looking alike because they were probably manufactured in China. The men stopped for a few moments and looked out to sea as they lit cigarettes. They chattered on, speaking Chinese in low voices just at the edge of Wilson's hearing, and then sauntered on along a dirt path, apparently on a routine sweep around the exterior of the property. Wilson wondered why Wong had a security patrol out so far from their construction site, but perhaps they were worried about people like him spying on their operation.

After the men left, Wilson watched the comings and goings of trucks to and from the site below. Semitrailers delivered and picked up sea containers every once in a while, and other supply trucks made deliveries frequently. Several gravel trucks brought crushed rock for use in concrete production. It seemed like any other construction site, except that one of the containers delivered was routed to the rear of the property and dropped off next to the locked containers as he watched. Three men dressed in uniforms different from those worn by the security guards stepped out of the warehouse at the rear of the property to receive and sign for the new container. Then the delivery truck left the premises.

Wilson dropped down and found the path the men had being following. It ran along the slope about a hundred yards from the perimeter fence at the back of the property. He walked along the path where it curved around and dropped down the slope toward the area where the locked containers were located. He made a mental note that this could be a route that would bring him nearer to the fence for a closer look at those containers. That would have to wait until a more opportune time. He walked west along the path until he could cut up through the trees, finding his original ridge trail again.

Wilson wondered why that set of containers had been placed at the rear of the property. Lightchurch, who was in direct contact with elements of the Grenada government, said they suspected some form of tax evasion. That was because all materials used for the construction project were exempt from normal import duties that are imposed on all products entering the country. They thought the construction company might be smuggling other commercial goods past customs. Lightchurch and Wilson suspected more sinister purposes for the subterfuge.

Back on the ridge, Wilson walked quickly toward Quarantine Point. It was nearly noon, and he wanted to check out the views of the construction site from that vantage point, if it was visible at all. He walked along the Morne Rouge Road and continued onto the point where that track diverged from the road. Clouds were beginning to form overhead, a sign that an afternoon storm could be brewing.

At Quarantine Point, he looked eastward along the coast and Grand Anse Beach, waves breaking in uniform rows on the golden sand. He could just make out the construction site on the forested slope above the west end of the beach. It did not provide him with much additional insight into the operation there. He felt stymied by the secrecy of the construction activity. *What were they doing on the site besides constructing a hotel?*

He crossed over to the other side of the point where a lookout provided an overview of Morne Rouge Bay. It was a beautiful, deep embayment, bracketed by black volcanic cliffs on both sides of the channel and running back to a black sand beach near a resort. He had walked that beach a few days before and had lunch at the resort's beach bar. It was a quiet setting.

What surprised him was the presence of a tall sailing yacht anchored at the mouth of the bay. It had not been there on his previous visit. It was an amazing sailing ship based on its size— at least two hundred feet long, with a boat launch on its stern for smaller craft. It had three tall masts, each at least 120 feet tall, and a modern, sleek design. The white hull was eye-catching on the blue Caribbean water. It was the sort of yacht that spoke of luxury and money. Its name on its stern was *Varoushka*.

As he watched, two men launched a Zodiac from the stern, and they powered away to the beach. Another man stood in the shade on the aft cockpit holding a rifle. At first Wilson thought it odd that the man had a weapon, then he saw the man move forward on the deck with a precision that comes only from military training. When the man stepped into the light, Wilson saw that the rifle was an assault weapon and that the man must therefore be a guard. That meant the owner of the yacht was not only wealthy but also had reason to need protection. Diving tanks on the rear ship's deck suggested they were there for reef diving, a great sport on the island. Wilson wondered who the owner could be and what he was doing in Morne Rouge Bay. *Varoushka* suggested a wealthy Russian owner.

Wilson checked his watch; it was almost 1:00 p.m. He started back toward Grand Anse for a meeting. He jogged along the road, going from tree to tree and staying under their umbra as much as possible in the rising heat and humidity of the day. He reached Morne Rouge Road and shortly came upon the driveway of the Cinnamon Tree Inn, where he was meeting a contact who he hoped could help him with a difficult issue.

***

Upon mounting the steps to the bar with its ceiling fans and cool tiles, he heard a familiar voice. "Wilson! Over here."

He made his way past several small decorated tables to the bar where a burly fellow sat wearing a blue jacket and a captain's hat, his trademark for the tourist business. Frank "Jimmy"

Pendergast, called "Captain Jimmy" by most people, was a robust man of about fifty years, a former member of the US Marines, and presently the owner, operator, and main force behind Reefer Scuba Diving Adventures. He was six feet five inches tall and muscular from years of military training and rough living; he also spoke three languages. He was bigger than life and had a huge laugh that was recognizable from across the room or even far away along the beach. The cap covered his shaved head, something he rarely displayed, except when diving. He was the man to know if you needed information about shipping and any activities along the seacoast.

"Hi, Jimmy!" Wilson called across the room as he approached the adjacent barstool and shook the man's big paw of a hand. "You're starting a little early, aren't you?" He pointed to Pendergast's mai tai on the counter.

"The sun has set over the yardarm somewhere in the world. Why don't you join me?" He called the barman over and ordered a refill on his drink. "I'm done with diving for the day anyway."

Wilson ordered a Stag beer and suggested they move to an out-of-the-way table for their conversation. He hoped that Pendergast had important information to share with him. Privacy would be essential.

When his beer came, they migrated to a small table at the edge of the open-air deck that had a fine view of a short stretch of Grand Anse Beach close to where Pendergast had his dock. Wilson asked, "Were you able to find out much about our friends on the freighter?"

Pendergast gave Wilson a quick evaluation, probably seeing how eager he was for the information. "Well, yes and no."

"I've heard that before. It usually isn't good news."

"Don't jump to any conclusions," Pendergast said. "My sources tell me the freighter unloaded several containers four weeks ago and then sailed away for a few days. They've been anchored where they are now for at least three weeks, doing nothing much except maintenance." He sipped his drink. "At least that's what they say they've been doing." He raised his eyebrows.

"That seems like a lot of maintenance at anchorage. They should be in dock for something that extensive."

"Precisely my thinking. They send a boat ashore twice a week for supplies, food, and miscellaneous stuff. But the amount of fresh food seems inordinately large for a crew of fifteen, which is what they list as their complement."

"How much?"

"Maybe enough for forty or fifty men, though I don't know how they keep them out of sight." Pendergast rubbed his chin and stared at his companion. "I wonder why they would have so many men on board, even if they are some sort of listening ship."

"Wait," Wilson said. "Do you have any info that supports that? I mean, I thought they might be doing electronic eavesdropping, but I have no proof except the inordinate number of antennas on the ship. And why station a listening ship in plain view of the entire bay?"

"One of my people says they purchased several electronic devices in Saint George's—a digital amplifier, some chips, and a few other things out of the ordinary—not repair material for most ship's systems." He paused for effect. "They also picked up a shipment of electronics at the marine terminal. A crate that was rushed airfreight from Caracas. My source said it was listed as electronic testing equipment—at least that's what the customs form said."

"What happened to the containers?" Wilson swigged his beer as he listened intently. "Were they routed to Wong Construction?"

"Good guess." Pendergast made a surreptitious scan of the tables nearby before he continued. "I have a list of serial numbers here." He tapped his jacket pocket, then slowly removed a sheet of paper folded twice like a business letter, and slid it across the table to Wilson. "The equipment in each container is also listed there, for what it's worth."

Wilson looked over the listing and frowned. "I doubt that this is all metal framing for the warehouse out at their site." He paused and sipped his beer. "The weights are rather high, even for construction supplies."

"Can't help you there." Pendergast signaled the barman for another round. "What else can I do for you?"

Wilson thought for a moment. "What do you know about the huge yacht over in Morne Rouge Bay?

Pendergast leaned forward. "She's a real beauty, isn't she? I'd like to look her over and see what she's got below decks." He paused. "The *Varoushka* is of Russian registration, owned by Boris Lavanenko, the Russian oligarch—apparently a close friend of President Petrov himself. So that means rich and powerful. He's the money behind RUS Industries, a big electronics and software company in Russia."

"RUS?" Wilson said. "Aren't they the people with the upgrade contract at the airport?"

"One and the same. Maybe he's here for the completion of the work for Maurice Bishop." He stared down at the beach and seemed to notice something happening there. He stood up and looked over the deck railing. "Odd for someone that important to oversee a rather limited contract. Don't you think?"

"Maybe he has a special interest in this job," Wilson said as he rubbed his jaw. "Have you or any of your friends seen him or know where he's staying? On his ship?"

"I think he sleeps on board, but I can ask around and see what else I can come up with." Pendergast looked down at the beach again, and he seemed suddenly concerned. "Say, I think I need to get down to the shop. I see a boat scanning our dock, and I better see what they're after."

He got up and threw forty Eastern Caribbean dollars on the table. "I'll let you know what I find out." With that, he walked briskly to the door and down the steps. Wilson saw him run toward the path that descended to the beach and his shop below.

Wilson lingered at the Cinnamon Tree as he finished his beer and enjoyed the view of the sea and beach below. He thought that this was one of the most pleasant postings he had been at in his short career as an agent. The island and the people beat his hometown of Chicago by a mile, except that he missed the jazz clubs he had frequented regularly. But after moving around on assignments so often, he found the Caribbean the closest thing to home for him. He relished the laidback atmosphere of the islands. He enjoyed doing what he did for the agency, and he was able to keep at his vocation as a writer and historian between assignments. What could be better?

He sipped the last of his beer and left twenty Eastern Caribbean dollars on the table. There was work to be done, and he had much to accomplish in a short time.

Chapter 4

Wednesday

Back at the hotel, Wilson finished comparing the list of containers he had seen at the Wong site with the lists he had received from Lightchurch and Pendergast. Many of the numbers on the open, actively used containers were on Lightchurch's list, so they seemed legitimate construction supplies. None of the containers from the back of the site were on either list. He quickly compiled a list of numbers for the ones at the back of the lot and sent it off in an encrypted email to Lightchurch, sharing what he had discovered. Maybe he could find out if any of those numbers belonged to other shipments made to the island by other means or by other parties. He also indicated in the email that he would like to see what was inside the suspicious containers, perhaps under cover of night. He wondered what Lightchurch thought of such a maneuver.

He did some research online about Boris Lavanenko. He was closely allied with Petrov in Russia and was suspected by some intelligence agencies of doing some of Petrov's dirty work. He certainly shared business investments with Petrov and had vacationed at his summer home on the Black Sea several times. They appeared to be old friends.

He also looked into the business interests of Wong Construction and learned that it was not only a construction company but also the construction arm of the Chinese trading and shipping giant World Electrosystems LTD, which was itself a subsidiary of Zangchung Industries, which was in turn a Chinese state-owned conglomerate with interests in far-flung locations around the world. Zangchung was the company most commonly chosen by the Chinese government to execute large-scale construction projects around Asia and in countries where China had long-term strategic interests. Those interests usually revolved around the development of resources or trade with third-world nations that needed an economic boost and willingly worked with the Chinese toward that goal, such as their Belt and Road Initiative. One of their recent joint military and commercial projects was located near Djibouti on the horn of Africa, where they would have access to the most important sea trade routes from Asia to the Mediterranean.

Wilson then went through his emails and sent a brief summary of events to his control via 256-bit encrypted email. It was nearly 7:00 p.m. by that time, and his stomach growled from neglect. He shut down his computer using the standard protocol and walked to the hotel's beach bar.

He nodded to Gordon as he entered the bar and pointed to a table near the rear of the dining area. He walked to the table and sat down. The bar was nearly full of diners and drinkers, more than usual on a Tuesday night, but perhaps not surprising with the election only seven days away. Many of the usual hotel guests were present, and he nodded to one or two he had spoken with on occasion.

One was a journalist named Tim Martin with the *Miami Observer*. He and Wilson had discussed the local election situation, and the man was sure that the opposition party would win the election. Martin had spent some time in the field with Hjarad Senjai's supporters in the GPC. He was impressed by their organization and funding. He was working on the money angle behind the election. Wilson needed to talk to him again and find out what he had learned. He waved Martin over for a drink and a chat.

Martin was already inebriated, which seemed to be his normal state when he had no deadline to meet. He also had a healthy expense account, so Wilson let him buy the drinks most of the time. It went with his cover of being a fellow journalist there working the election story. Wilson's angle on the election was the socioeconomic effect on the nation as it entered a new chapter in its history. He had used the cover to ask many people about the election and what it meant for the islanders and their economy.

Martin arrived at the table at the same moment that Gordon brought Wilson's rum and ginger ale. Martin slouhed into the chair across from Wilson and ordered another rum punch before Gordon left the table. Martin had developed a love for the hotel's rum punches, which were loaded with a devastating pour of four different rums and a small amount of mixed fruit juice. In any case, it made him a very jovial man and a good sport.

"Wilson, old man, how are you?" He reached out his hand and shook briefly with his sweaty palm. "You're not afraid of the volcano, are you?"

"Have you heard anymore about the eruption?"

"No, just that it's proceeding deep underwater. I guess a local freighter ran right into the exclusion zone yesterday and saw the sea rising up on him. He turned tail in time to float out of it." Martin took a sip of rum punch and smiled. "I wrote a short piece about it for the paper, but my damn editor said no one would possibly care about a freighter in this hell hole of a country." He laughed but then stopped and looked worried. "I wonder if I have a future with the *Observer*. They're so shortsighted and want only to please millennials these days," he mused as he sloshed punch down his hatch.

"I missed that. I've been buried in documents today and have several meetings tomorrow with government types. It will be another dull day, I'm afraid." Wilson liked to build up the shear boredom of his research and writing, keeping Martin from asking too much about it. As it happened, he did have a few meetings at Government House the next day, and some of that would be tedious. Fortunately, Martin carried the conversation while Gordon returned with more drinks and took Wilson's dinner order. Martin decided to join him for the meal and ordered the grilled mahi-mahi, the same as Wilson.

"I was out today with my friends at the GPC hustings in the Saint Andrew North Parish. They're very charged up about the election and were plastering those awful orange posters everywhere. They had a whole pickup truck full of the damn things and were stapling them to almost every light pole. Even on shop walls and windows. I asked how they could afford so many of them, and they said they didn't know but they loved the action. One of the fellows told me that no one seemed to know why they had so much money available, but they were happy for it. They feel they have a chance at winning this time around. And they get free drinks sometimes too. A hell of a party."

"No wonder they have so many volunteers. Free beer is a great incentive to knock on doors."

"But that's just it. It truly seems that nobody knows where the money has come from. One of the district leaders said she heard it was from lots of small donations, especially from Grenadians who live overseas. But I doubt that. I mean, I saw a sheet with part of their budget, and it seems way more than the average person could contribute, even if they were doing well overseas." Martin ordered yet another rum punch and finished his meal with a burp. "Damn fine fish they have here in Grand Anse. It'll be a shame to go home after the election."

"I wonder if you could talk to one of the people at campaign headquarters about their fund-raising. Maybe you could get a look at the books. Say you need it for your story." Wilson planted the thought in Martin's head. "That would be a great story—a real scoop if you got the dope on the campaign financing."

"That's a great idea. I do know someone who could probably get me a look-see. And she owes me now." Martin hesitated. "I think I could get the information but . . . it's just that I'm not very good with numbers and accounting. I probably couldn't figure it out very well."

Wilson saw an opportunity. "Well, if that's all you're worried about, I could probably help. I mean, if I don't have a deadline. I could help you review the documents or files, if that would be useful to you." He hesitated and then went on. "It might even help me in my work too. But I don't know. It might pull me away from my article." He didn't want to appear too eager.

"Would you be willing to help?" Martin leaned in, hopeful and even anxious. "I would be greatly in your debt. It could be just the thing to get me noticed back at the old Borg ship we call the *Observer*. Maybe my editor would be impressed enough to keep me in Miami once in a while." Martin suddenly seemed despondent. He stood up from the table, and his face turned a shade of green and white at the same time.

Martin fled the restaurant, headed toward the bathroom in the hallway. Several people in the bar noticed his departure and laughed. It was not the first time he had gotten sick on rum punch.

A news headline flashed on the television screen over the bar, and one of the barmen turned up the volume. "This report just in. Mr. Neville Charles, the National Standard Party's candidate for minister from West Saint George's who was injured in an electoral riot yesterday, has been transferred by air ambulance to Port of Spain, Trinidad, for further treatment. His injuries include a concussion and other serious damages that require the care of specialists who cannot be found here in Grenada. It appears that he will not be able to continue his campaign for office under the present conditions." Then a political ad for Mr. Charles's opponent in the election ran twice sequentially along with the GBTV disclaimers. The barman switched the television to the in-house music source, Stingray, which played the current hit R&B single by Khalid, "Young Dumb & Broke." Several people in the bar sang along with the catchy tune about a down-and-out youth who had no clue.

Gordon worked his way over to the table with another rum and ginger ale for Wilson. "Mr. Wilson, dey beat him up real bad. An' you hear what else? Six of the men they arrested were Venezuelans and two were Cubans. Now what they doin' protestin' in our election? And beatin' people?"

"Really?" Wilson thought about it a moment and frowned. "Gordon, that should surprise me, but somehow it fits in with other stories I've been told about the election. I haven't heard that on the TV yet. How did you find out?"

"I heard it from some NSP folks. I hear about stuff all the time from customers who work on the NSP campaigns. They come in here and say somethin' ain't right about this year. Someone broke into the campaign office for south Saint George's and vandalized the place. Sprayed orange paint on T-shirts, posters, an' everything. Lucky no one was there and got hurt, dey say."

"It sounds like things are getting pretty rough, all right. Can't the police do anything?"

"I don't know. I just feel it's getting real bad—real bad." He looked up as Mr. Morant entered the bar. "I gotta go." Gordon hurried away and intercepted Morant at the bar.

Just then Wilson's cell phone vibrated with a call from an unlisted number. It rang four times, then stopped. He waited until the same number called back. "Hello. What can I do for you?"

Darius Lightchurch spoke softly. "Need to meet ASAP. Can you come to Umbrellas right away?"

Wilson looked around the bar. "Yes, give me fifteen."

The line went dead.

Wilson wondered what that was about. He stood up and caught Gordon's attention. Then he made a writing gesture in the air, indicating he wanted his bill. Gordon nodded and walked over with the hotel receipt for his signature. "See you later, Mr. Wilson."

Wilson turned to walk to his room and bumped directly into a young woman who held a glass of white wine in her hand. On impact, the wine splashed up onto her blouse, and she immediately began wiping it off with her fingers in rapid sweeping motions. "*¡Dios mio!*" she said. "Oh shit." Then she looked up into Wilson's face. "You spilled my wine, señor."

She stared at him like it was his fault, and maybe it was. She had wide-set brown eyes and a bronze complexion beneath light-brown hair, pulled to the side in a ponytail. Wilson was taken in by her good looks but felt he couldn't really be blamed for the accident. "I'm sorry. I didn't see you there."

"I guess I should have been more careful." She smiled then with plump red lips, forming dimples in her cheeks. It was a refreshing smile. "Sorry, did I get any on you?"

"No, I seem unscathed," Wilson said as she checked his shirt for damage. "But I'm sorry too. It's a shame to waste good wine. Chardonnay, was it?"

"Yes, it was." She smiled again, ready to let the incident go. Then she seemed to make a decision as her expression changed. "I'm so sorry. Where are my manners?" She stuck out her hand like a Realtor ready for business. "I'm Tori Vargas. I'm here with the economic conference." Her pleasant voice carried a moderate Venezuelan accent.

Instinctively, Wilson took her hand and shook it. "I'm Robert Wilson. I'm a reporter and historian. I'm writing about the election and how things work here in Grenada." He smiled cautiously. "Pleased to meet you."

"Oh, how interesting," she said. "Maybe we can talk a little about your work?"

"And I could buy you another glass of wine to make up for the spillage." He grinned at the obvious pickup line. "I would love to do just that, but I'm late for a meeting." He watched as a frown appeared on her face. "But maybe I could take a rain check and then you could tell me about this conference you're attending. What do you say?"

She thought about it for all of three seconds and then smiled again. "Yes, that would be very nice, Mr. Wilson—Roberto. Maybe later tonight? I have a session but will be finished at ten."

"I think I can do that. If not, I'll call and leave a message with Gordon at the bar."

"OK." She nodded her head as she checked her watch. "I must go too. *Hasta la vista*. See you later." She bustled out of the bar toward the meeting rooms at the west conference center. Wilson watched her walk away with interest and then departed quickly for the side gate of the hotel property.

***

When he arrived at the beachside bar and restaurant called Umbrellas, it was very busy. Soca music was playing, and a lot of people were shouting and having a good time. The usual contingent of medical students was there, partying and celebrating something; perhaps they passed an exam that day and could risk the loss of gray matter due to excess alcohol consumption. He was always amazed that med students could put away so much booze in one night.

He entered the main building where the bar was located and immediately saw Madeline sitting glamorously at one of the tall tables, dressed as if on a dinner date. He wasn't sure if he should approach her and reveal that they knew each other, but she solved that problem by calling his name. "Robert! Over here."

He stepped to the table and was surprised when she got to her feet, came over, and gave him a warm hug, something she would not normally do. He felt her slender body press against him. She whispered, "Pretend we're on a first date. Don't hug too long." Her muscles tightened, and she pulled away after a few seconds. "And watch your hands."

"Where's our friend?"

"He's outside in the Rover. Pretend we're going somewhere else for dinner. We'll walk outside together in two minutes, OK?"

"You look lovely tonight. Have you eaten already?"

"Yes, we were at a function earlier, so I nibbled on the hors d'oeuvres."

"But who is with him now? You're his main protector, aren't you?"

"We have a driver tonight, and his lordship has upped his security." She looked at her watch and stood to leave.

They sauntered out of Umbrellas, she leading and he with a hand to her back at appropriate moments at the stairs. She led him around the corner of the building to the side street that connected to the main beach road. A large black Land Rover was silhouetted about a hundred yards along the road. It pulled forward as they approached, and the two passenger-side doors opened. Madeline pushed Wilson toward the rear door, and she stepped into the front seat. He got in and greeted Lightchurch, who occupied the other side of the back seat.

"Good seeing you, Robert. Hope I didn't inconvenience you with the late notice."

"No, Darius. What else would I be doing tonight?"

"This is my driver and new security man, Nash. He's cleared for anything we might discuss, same as Madeline."

"Nice to meet you, Nash." A nod of the driver's head in response.

"Let's get down to it," said Lightchurch. "I was disturbed by the list of container numbers you sent me. I had one of my people run the numbers through the database, and according to the results, those containers were never handled here on Grenada. So something is amiss. Someone may be bringing in containers without going through the main port or the customs process."

"But how could that happen? It takes a heavy-lift crane to offload a container. They weigh too much to handle any other way," Wilson said. "As far as I know, there's only one port with those kind of cranes—Saint George's harbor. The containers must have come in through the port."

"Exactly my thinking, but someone has failed to record those containers, circumventing customs." Lightchurch twisted sideways in his seat. "The question is who and why?"

"It seems that someone in the dockworkers union must be involved if there were so many discrepancies." Wilson considered the implications. "One or two errors might be a recording issue, but this seems deliberate and therefore malicious. We must get to the bottom of it—and soon."

"The union is completely under the control of the GPC. They're constantly supporting each other, even in this election. They're all in Hjarad Senjai's pocket."

"If we knew what was inside those containers, we would know what's intended. From that, we can deduce who is importing the containers." Wilson thought out loud. "But we need to find the containers and figure that out. The locked containers on the Wong job site might be the best starting point."

"It would be difficult to get past their security patrols and access the containers," Madeline commented. "Could take some planning."

Wilson looked at her and smiled. She returned a conspiratorial grin. "Perhaps a diversion? Keep the guards occupied?"

"Maybe it could be arranged." Wilson thought out loud. "Two people could get inside the perimeter. A disturbance of some kind out front, noisy and potentially dangerous to the job site."

"Plastic explosives could cut open the locks and doors," Lightchurch suggested.

"Too loud. It would attract the guards . . . Bolt cutters, big ones. And weapons."

Lightchurch leaned toward Wilson. "That's why you need Madeline and me—to get it done."

"Can we get help from the police?"

"I wouldn't know who to ask for help under these conditions. We can't trust anyone in the current government."

"We'll have to make do." Wilson looked at Lightchurch. "I'll run it past my control. Do I have your support, Darius?"

"Yes, and I insist that Madeline be your number two on this. She can get you any items that you'll need. Shall we begin planning now? And you two can work out the details tomorrow."

"Can we pull this off by tomorrow night, Madeline?" Wilson asked.

"It'll be close. Let's see how the plan comes together." Her face drew tight as she focused on the task at hand. "The diversion might take more time to set up."

"Let me make a phone call and then I have time to work on it now." He stepped out of the car and made a call to Gordon at the hotel bar.

Chapter 5

Thursday

Wilson rose early the next morning. To avoid a traffic jam, he rode the number one bus into downtown Saint George's to the office of the election commission. They were located in one of the gray government structures built on the old botanical gardens property. He was one of about a dozen journalists and three dozen other interested parties who had come to hear about the preparations for the upcoming election.

The matronly woman in charge began with a long list of introductions of people who were in the smallest way involved in the elections. He could see that everyone was extremely proud of the effort made to get this election right. Grenada was widely known for conducting fair and accountable elections, perhaps having the best record of any government in the Caribbean and Central America.

The guests of honor at the meeting were the seven poll watchers who had been sent by the Organization of American States, or OAS; they asked several questions as the presentation went on. Finally, the woman told the assembled press and others that there would actually be two elections: one on Sunday, three days before the main event on Tuesday. The Sunday election was held just for law enforcement officers, who would be unable to vote on Tuesday because they would be hard at work maintaining the peace on Election Day itself.

Then a man, Mr. Chambers, stood up and made the technical presentation of the actual vote-counting machines that would be used. This was the part of the story that Wilson was interested in. For the first time in history, Grenada was going to use automated ballot-counting machines for voting. The voters would use traditional pencils to mark their preferences on a paper ballot, and their ballots would be numbered so that voters would get a receipt tied to their ballots. They could then validate their votes if there should be any question of the accuracy of the ballot count. The ballots themselves would be scanned through a device that would then tally the results and present them to the electoral board, who would supervise it all. When satisfied that all ballots had been cast and counted, the board would certify the election results. Then everyone on the winning side would be happy, and the losers would protest as usual.

The technical man demonstrated how it all worked by passing out sample ballots with fictitious names on them to all participants. The audience was then told to mark their choices with pencils and to tear off the small strip at the bottom of the ballot for their records. He collected the ballots and ran them through the machine for a count. He told everyone the results, and they were instantly displayed on a computer monitor. It went quite smoothly.

Wilson then asked him a question. "Excuse me, but I wonder how you verify any one single ballot. I mean, suppose I have my receipt and I want to see that my vote was counted correctly. Can that be done?"

Chambers responded the way all bureaucrats answer questions anywhere in the world. "Yes, excellent question. I was hoping someone would ask this because it is just what makes this voting process so vital." He smiled and walked over to Wilson. "Sir, do you have the identification strip from your ballot?"

He reached out and took the strip, then showed everyone on the computer screen as he typed in the ID number for that ballot. The screen then called up a complete image of the ballot and showed a summary of the actual votes for the ballot just below the image. The scan and the data matched. Everyone in the room applauded when they saw how it worked. It was impressive.

Chambers said, "It makes verification of a ballot very simple. And if you must rerun a set of ballots from a single ballot box, you can do that and compare the results of each count independently. We're doing just that to the results for the Sunday voting, just to be sure everything is running correctly. Of course we won't release those results until the full Tuesday ballot results are complete and then we'll mix the police votes into each appropriate parish or precinct." He paused and looked around the room for questions, answering a few before the meeting broke up.

Wilson walked to the front of the room and asked about taking a picture of one of the voting machines. He was allowed to do so, as were others. He also noted the name and model of the machine. He even noticed that the serial number for the machine was printed on a strip at the backside of the device. He wrote it down. He thanked the commissioners for their presentation and then walked down to the main road where he caught a bus back to Grand Anse.

The bus was crowded with schoolchildren on the return trip because they'd had only a half day of classes. When they entered the bus, all the little boys and girls, from six to fifteen years of age, said, "Good morning." Most of the fellow bus riders responded in kind, even making places for the youngsters to sit comfortably. It was nice seeing so many polite people in one place.

***

When he arrived at the hotel, Leslie greeted him as he passed through the gate. "Another good day, Mr. Wilson."

"Yes, it looks like fine weather. Hardly a cloud in the sky."

"Don't be fooled, Mr. Wilson. Dey say we may get a soakin' tonight." Wilson had learned in a short time that Leslie was a better predictor of the weather than the GSTV weatherman.

"Oh, you think so? I was going for a hike later this afternoon."

"You be fine with an umbrella this afternoon, but tonight it come like raining frogs. You'll see."

Wilson went to his room and began researching the voting machines and their manufacturer. They were model 156-B of the Votadigit Company of Minneapolis, Minnesota. They had a good track record with several election commissions in various states in the US and Canada. There were even testimonials by researchers and others.

He dug into the ownership of the company and found out little other than that the company had been sold three years before to a conglomerate that included many electronics companies and makers of technical instruments. He decided to send the information he had back to Langley so that someone else could research it, his time being limited due to other events. He sent it off in an encrypted email.

While online, he noted that Langley had responded to his message the night before. He opened it and was angry that, instead of an answer, he had received more questions about the surveillance he had proposed.

He sat back and thought about the mission that he and Madeline were planning for later that night. He had described it as surveillance to minimize this sort of bureaucratic second-guessing of his plans. He did mention that he was coordinating with Lightchurch's people and that they were on board with it. He did not mention that it involved trespassing, breaking and entering, and possible use of weapons. If he brought all that up, it would be stuck in bureaucratic limbo until Christmas. Like all good agents, he realized it was better to limit knowledge of his operations until they were over. Then if they went well, he would share the results. Otherwise, nothing would ever get done.

The agency had also responded to his request for background information about Madeline Caron. He had asked for her training and operational status as an agent for Grenada. After all, he would be going into the field with her and needed to know her capabilities.

He opened the dossier the agency had on her and found it illuminating. She was a well-trained operative with eleven years' experience in Grenada and other Commonwealth nations. She was born in Grenada thirty-one years ago, the daughter of a prominent business family. She had excelled in school and won scholarships to study in England. She had been an athlete at university in swimming and some track and field events. She had studied at Oxford University and was apparently recruited there. She received training at the British Intelligence Agency, but no details were given. There was mention of several covert assignments, but details were classified. His impression was that she was a highly qualified professional, and he was glad to have her on their team.

He decided to respond minimally to the agency's questions and to mislead them as much as possible about when things would happen. He would not touch his emails until the mission was over.

He had just enough time to walk to the bar and flag Gordon for a table before the charming Ms. Vargas arrived. She was wearing a stylish broad-brimmed straw hat, a bikini barely covered by a beach wrap, and sequined flip-flops. She was breathtaking, and many heads turned to take in her visage and sleek form.

"Roberto, I am so happy that you suggested lunch today instead of drinks last night." She sat down next to him and took off her hat, placing it carefully on the extra chair beside her. "I was very tired by the time the sessions finished yesterday, and I would have been boring company."

"Yes, I was out quite late myself. I would not have made interesting conversation either." He eyed her bathing suit. "You didn't attend the conference this morning?"

"Oh, I went to the first lecture but decided I could not be so close to this beautiful beach and only work. So I swam and sat in the sun a little." She leaned forward and brought her tanned shoulders close for him to examine. "Here, feel my skin. It is still hot from the sun." She was very coy about it and let him touch her delicate bronze. "You see, I feel nice, don't I?" A devilish grin.

"Yes, Ms. Vargas. You are definitely hot." He smiled as she blushed just the right amount to show her pleasure.

"Call me Tori."

"Tori, shall we order drinks?" He waved to Gordon, who approached their table. "Maybe a rum punch? Have you tried them here? They're very tasty. A friend of mine swears by them."

"Oh, that sounds delicious." Gordon left to fill their drink order.

"What will you have? Shall we eat lunch or just talk for a while?" Tori was all smiles, a vivacious companion.

"Let's eat something light, shall we? Maybe one of their crab salads or an empanada?" He hoped she would choose a simple meal. He must move on to other things in the afternoon.

"Oh yes. Crab salad sounds very nice, Roberto. Will you have the same?" She reached over and touched his arm as he searched the simple lunch menu. "Then you can tell me what it is you are writing about."

Gordon appeared at the table with two rum punches, and they ordered their food. Wilson led her in a toast and then said, "Tell me about your conference first. Is it about economics in Venezuela or about some economic topics that apply everywhere?"

"Oh, I see." She straightened up in her chair and worry lines appeared around her eyes as she composed her thoughts. "It's about both. You know our economy is not doing very well right now, but that is because the United States has cut off much of our banking access to world markets. The great leader will overcome these problems, but it is very difficult. The lectures are about how we can work around some of the conflicts with the US banking system and other issues." She finished and uttered a sigh of relief, now that she had done her patriotic duty defending the indefensible.

"I see." Wilson almost felt sorry for her and her unfortunate position. "It must be difficult to keep positive under those conditions. Are you giving a paper here or just attending the conference?"

"I am just a facilitator for the conference," she said prettily. "I am here to make sure that everything goes well and that people behave. I am sort of a chaperone for some of the attendees."

"Oh, really? Do they need watching over?"

"Yes, they do. Some might try to stay here longer than they are allowed to." She looked worried. "I mean . . ."

"You mean they might get an offer to work somewhere else?" He tried helping her out. "Get recruited by another company or government?"

She looked relieved, the worry retreating from her face. "Yes, that's it. I am supposed to look for anyone who has too much interest in our people—for just that reason. We can't have our best people stolen away or our secrets compromised." She scooted her chair a little closer to his and reached for his arm again.

He wondered if anyone would really hire any of these people who had managed to drive a thriving economy into the ditch so badly. No one would hire them. But the Venezuelans might try defecting to the United States, as so many of their countrymen had already done. It was like the old Iron Curtain days when the USSR had minders keeping their citizens from running away to the West. Chavez and Maduro had created the same type of socialist dictatorship with extensive help from the Cubans, those models of world citizenship.

Wilson caught Gordon's eye and ordered more drinks. Tori slurped down the remainder of her first tasty rum punch. They carried on a pleasant conversation while he sipped his punch and Tori gulped down two more. She began giggling by that time and became more forward in her manner toward him.

He wondered if it was her assignment to get him involved in a personal relationship. She certainly acted like it was a setup and that he might be a target. Or was he getting ahead of himself? Maybe she was just a lonely woman who never got out of the country and so was having a good time for herself. In either case, her beach wrap had slipped down, revealing more than enough cleavage to interest any man walking by at the bar and holding Gordon's attention when he came over, checking on them frequently. She seemed genuine in her behavior, or perhaps she was not a scripted professional who was used to seducing men for their secrets. At least not as a profession.

Wilson did learn some interesting things from Vargas. A few people at the conference were real economists. Many of the other people attending the conference were in fact security personnel. They had rented a conference room at the Hempstead, and some staffers like Vargas had rooms there. Most of the other Venezuelans were staying at a hotel farther down the beach that offered cheaper rooms but few other facilities. The people staying there had to double up or triple up on rooms. Many of them did not attend the meetings, like at many conferences everywhere, but spent the time sightseeing instead. They had rented a sports facility for two weeks, but Vargas said she did not know why. After so many drinks, she had become sleepy and chatty about her personal life and the difficulties of living in Caracas as a single woman. She was an engaging person. He felt sorry for her troubled life in Venezuela.

Wilson checked his watch. He had to leave by 2:00 p.m., meet Madeline, and continue preparing for their excursion that night. Suddenly, having a romantic lunch with Vargas and pumping her for information seemed a poor use of his time.

"Say, Tori," he said brightly. "Maybe it's a good time to move somewhere else."

She seemed to like the idea. "We could go to my room. I have a bottle of rum there. I could change into something more comfortable." She raised her eyebrows and gave him a suggestive curve of her lips.

He signed for the lunch and stood up, helping her to unsteady feet. Three rum punches were way past her usual lunch intake. They wobbled out of the bar and toward the other wing of the hotel where she said she had a room, number 319. They found their way there slowly, stopping to admire the bougainvillea she liked, and then stood outside her room as she dug in her beach bag for the key. Once the door was open, he helped her inside and she turned toward him for a kiss. He intercepted her and gave her a hug instead, but he got a wet kiss on his neck as they turned.

Then she passed out in his arms, and he dragged her to the bed. He tripped on a huge, square, green-flowered suitcase and nearly fell on top of her. He placed her on the bed, ensuring that she would not roll off the side in her sleep. She looked very happy and relaxed as she lay there, a smile on her lips.

She was out cold, so he took a moment to snoop around the room. He checked her purse and found that her driver's license and passport identified her as Tori Vargas, employee of the Venezuela Department of Social Information. It sounded like the propaganda arm of the government, which fit her role at the conference. He found nothing more nefarious than that, except for a sheet of paper listing the conference venues, including the rented sports facility. He shot a photo of it with his phone and replaced all the papers as they had been before.

She had fallen into a deep, drooling sleep.

He left the room and gently closed the door.

Chapter 6

Thursday

As Wilson drove slowly through the afternoon drizzle and the wet streets, he made the decision to move ahead with the operation for the break-in at the Wong job site. He still had no confirmation from Langley, but he felt he had no choice. His mission to Grenada had grown in scope from information gathering and analysis to active involvement in a timely and dangerous situation. The need to find out what was really happening forced him forward on his own without agency support on the ground. His only allies were an aging lord turned diplomat and a capable local agent named Madeline. Time was crucial. They had to risk the danger and solve the mystery that confronted them and, perhaps, the independence of this island nation. There was no turning back.

At 2:00 p.m. he arrived at a warehouse where Madeline was assembling gear they would need for their break-in to the Wong Construction site. He knocked on the rear door and then waited for her to open it for him.

The day was warming up into the low eighties. He wished he had worn shorts for the afternoon heat. At least the guayabera shirt kept him relatively cool.

"You're late, Robert." She looked outside to ensure that he had not been followed and then locked the door. "Come over here and see what I've been doing." She led him to a side table, sauntering along in shorts, a T-shirt, and flip-flops.

He stepped up to the table that was covered with small items. She looked at his face. "You have lipstick on your cheek.

Here." She threw him a shop cloth and grinned. "I hope your lunch was rewarding."

"It's not what you think. Vargas didn't have much information to share." He wiped his face and threw the cloth on the table. "Nice toys you have here."

Two Sig Sauer semiautomatic handguns with extra clips of 9mm ammo lay on the table, along with tactical vests and two sets of black clothing. Ski masks would be too hot to wear in this weather, so they had opted to blacken their faces and wear black ball caps instead. There were low-light photographic cameras and handheld radios. They had been set to rare frequencies that reconnaissance told them were not used by the Wong guards. Flashlights, flash-bang grenades, and rucksacks filled out the materials they would need.

"I had Nash drive over and sit by the site for a while last night and again this morning to verify the frequencies of the guard radios, so we should be good. We have pistols with forty rounds of ammo, even though we won't need them if all goes as planned."

"And the bolt cutters?"

"Over there." She pointed to the side of the room. A huge pair of cutters lay on the floor. He walked over to check them out and lifted them up. "Geez," he said. "These will do the job, but they'll be hard to conceal and drag through the brush." He tested the gape on the cutters. "They'll cut through those padlocks easy enough."

"I brought flash bangs in case we get in trouble, but I hope to hell we don't need them." She handled them carefully. "There are a few smoke grenades too."

"If we get caught with all this stuff, it will be impossible to claim we're just burglars." He laughed at the thought of two people dressed in black at night arguing that they were just stealing a few tools.

She stopped to look at him and then laughed too. "Right. So let's not get caught."

"My source says he can get about twenty people together at the front gate at nine p.m., and they can make a hell of a racket," Wilson said. "They'll start with a protest of the foreign company coming in and stealing local jobs. After thirty minutes, they'll start getting nasty and take it up to riot level. They'll even throw things at the guards and set a fire by the fence. That's when we must get in and get out. They'll disperse as soon as police reinforcements show up."

"So we'll have about twenty minutes for cutting the fence, dropping down, and taking a look. Good."

"But they can't get it organized until tomorrow night. We'll have to wait for it." Wilson was disappointed that they couldn't get into the containers until then. "We can use the extra time for surveillance and to make sure we know the site operations."

"Shit," Madeline said. She leaned her butt against the table's edge and crossed her arms over her chest, a disappointed look on her face. "Too bad. I'm up for it tonight. Shame to wait."

"I have something else we can do tonight. I found out that the Venezuelans have rented a building they're using for some sort of meeting place. Might be worth seeing what they're doing there."

"What do we care? They have their conference at the Hempstead, don't they?" she asked, irritated. "Why would they need another place for meetings?"

"I don't know, but I think there's more going on than just meetings. I've seen some of them at the Hempstead bar. They don't look like any economists I've seen before. Too young and fit. Vargas said some of them don't even go to the conference."

"That's odd. What about her? Is she an academic?" Madeline asked, one eyebrow cocked.

"No. That's just it." He stood and walked back and forth a few times before speaking again. "She said she's a minder. Not directly, but she's keeping tabs on people so they don't defect. They used that in the Eastern Block during the Cold War. So she's acting as part of the security team."

"Maybe that's why they have young men with them; security can keep an eye on the others."

"I asked at the hotel, and they said the Venezuelan conference takes a break for the weekend and then continues through Tuesday of next week. A long conference for seventy attendees."

"Seems suspicious, but maybe they have a lot of economic problems to discuss." She broke into a chuckle. "Hell, their economy needs all the help it can get."

Wilson laughed. "You seem to have everything ready here. I think I might go catch a certain marine at his shop. Call me if you need anything."

"I'll do a little surveillance at the Wong site tonight. Check on their schedule."

"Sounds like a plan."

***

"He should be back in an hour if you want to wait. He took out a group diving on the reef west of here. It shouldn't be long," Chris said. Chris "Wet Dog" Thatcher was Captain Jimmy's number two, his right-hand man. He had been a Navy Seal in his day but had adapted to the island lifestyle and married a local woman who he adored. He had been with Jimmy for nine years and ran half of the dives the company made. He had many stories to tell, most of which were still classified, if you believed his tales.

"I think I'll drive up to the point and watch for them from there." Wilson walked to the door. "I'll see you soon."

He headed to his car and out to the Morne Rouge Road. He drove up the hill, passing the Wong site as he went. There was a lot of activity, with trucks coming and going. Every third truck was a cement mixer. They must have been pouring a foundation to use so much concrete. He noticed that two trucks were bringing in fresh containers and one was hauling another away. He wondered where it was going.

He drove slowly to the little picnic area on Quarantine Point and parked. Then he walked out to the same viewpoint he had been at the day before. He saw the *Varoushka* in the same spot as before, a Zodiac just leaving with two men in diving gear on board and two other men, one driving the boat and one talking to the divers. They headed out to sea and then swung left to follow the coastline west.

He lay down in the shade for comfort during the long wait. A warm and gentle breeze blew over the point, ruffling the leaves of the trees and feeling pleasant on a warm day. He kept an eye out for Jimmy's dive boat and nearly fell asleep. He awoke just as Jimmy's thirty-foot Sportcraft rounded the point with seven or eight people on board.

He stretched and then sauntered to the car. He looked down at the *Varoushka* again as he did so and noticed that another boat, maybe a whaler, was tied up to the stern with four divers in wetsuits on board. The boat pulled away and headed out on the same course that the Zodiac had taken.

He arrived at Reefer Scuba Diving Adventures as Jimmy was saying goodbye to his customers. Wet Dog was accounting for all the gear they had used that day. Jimmy waved Wilson into his office and grabbed two Stag beers from the fridge on the way.

"Hell of a day diving. The sea was real clear out at Rum Runner. We saw some angelfish, and people got good photos. Can't get much better."

Wilson didn't know the site but took Jimmy's word for the venture's success. "Sounds great. I'm not much of a diver myself. Maybe I should go out with you one of these days."

"I know what you're thinking, but I haven't got much on the Russians yet. We did see them go out past Canoe Bay twice today." Jimmy took a swig of beer. "In fact, there were a couple of boats heading out as we came back in. We waved at the last crew, but they seemed like the sullen type. Great diving gear, though. I could see that from far off."

"I saw them loading four men on a boat just before you landed. Where are they going?"

"Don't know. But I got a man free tomorrow. I thought I'd send him out fishing to keep an eye on those Ruskies. They seem to be going around the point toward Shark Reef. That's interesting diving near there, and it can get deep farther out."

"Anything new on the containers?"

"No, but I'll keep you informed when I do." Jimmy jumped up. "Gotta go. Meeting some tour guides from a cruise ship in an hour and need to freshen up for my sales pitch." He laughed and then saw Wilson to his car.

Wilson drove along Morne Rouge Road and then crossed over to the airport road, looking for the address he had obtained from Tori Vargas's room. It took a few tries, but after he asked a man at the CTEC gas station, he found the building. It was once a meetinghouse of some sort, perhaps an indoor badminton venue, and it was in an area with few other active commercial properties around it.

There were several cars parked out front, and he could see a number of men standing in front of the building, smoking cigarettes and hanging out. He gave it a once-over as he drove by, not wanting to draw attention. He managed to find an empty lot nearby that gave him a view of the rear of the building. There was an ordinary backdoor and what looked like a former roll-up garage door. A man was standing beside the door wearing a uniform, apparently on guard. Wilson drove by on the way back to Grand Anse Road and took a photo of the building with his cell phone.

He thought it odd that the Venezuelans had rented a place far away from their conference hotel and near the airport. Maybe it was the best deal they could get. But what were they using it for?

He decided against returning to the hotel for dinner in case Tori Vargas appeared and made amorous overtures. Instead, he drove into Saint George's to the Nutmeg House, a fine eatery near the harbor. There was a traffic jam by the marina due to a political demonstration. He turned down a side street to get around it but then had trouble finding a place to park near the restaurant. Finally, he found a tiny space uphill from the Carenage, the inner harbor, and walked back three blocks to eat.

He had been to the Nutmeg before and favored their delicious beef roti, a spicy Indian dish of curried meat and potatoes wrapped in garlic naan. He ordered a Carib beer to wash it down and settled in for fine dining while looking out the window at the late-evening boat traffic in the harbor. It was dark, and the lights of the working ships and boats offered a picturesque view from the restaurant window.

As he finished his third beer, he heard loud noises coming from the street. The demonstration had migrated toward the downtown from the marina. Men and women shouted campaign slogans with megaphones, and many voices chanted the various songs of the GPC organization. It was very loud, and Wilson wondered if he would be able to drive back past the throng of human chaos. Some in the crowd were throwing stones at passing cars, and he saw a man ignite several torches for their numbers.

"Sir, you had better leave soon," the waiter named Clarence said. "The demonstration is headed for the market, and they may be very angry tonight." He stood by the table and craned his neck, watching the passing crowd. Suddenly a stone came through the open window and crashed against the wall on the far side of the room. "Get ready to go, sir. Forget the bill. Just leave now. You can pay me tomorrow."

The waiter waved his hand at the busboy, who came over to the table. "Here—Jamal will show you how to get past the mob. Hurry, sir, before they get drunk and break things." The man looked afraid, like he had seen this mischief before.

Wilson threw money on the table to cover his bill and hurried to the stairs, where the twelve-year-old Jamal waited, looking frightened. The boy ran down the stairs and stopped dead on the last step, surveying the dark street. Then he ran across the alleyway, as if he had some practice at sneaking about in the dark. A few men were already marching up the street, and they shouted at the two of them as they scurried along. As Wilson ran after the boy in the dark, he heard feet chasing behind them. He followed Jamal as closely as he could, staying ahead of their pursuers. But the boy knew where he was going and could make better speed.

They came to a cross street Wilson recognized. "My car is down here."

The boy stopped, eyes wide as he listened to the crowd gaining on them. He shouted, "Not that way, sir. Come like this." He ran into a dark alley with Wilson on his heels. The men who were chasing them ran past on the street as they crept along the pitch-black alley.

They turned and walked through the backyard of a small house and onto a dirt path. Wilson couldn't see where he was going and so had to trust the boy to know the way. They could hear men shouting in the streets around them. It sounded like the demonstration had turned into a mob that started to break windows and beat cars they encountered on the street. Wilson hoped Jamal could get him out of there safely. He began to fear what would happen if the mob caught them in the open.

They came out onto the street again, and Wilson saw his car. The street was dark and empty of people, but they could hear shouting and a megaphone only one block away. He opened the car door and started it while the boy stood lookout next to his door.

Wilson began pulling the car forward into the lane, but the boy pointed the other way. "You must go this way or you find mob." That was the wrong direction on the one-way street, but who cared. "Thank you, Jamal!" The boy knew how to get around the town, and he vanished into the night within seconds.

Wilson pulled away with no lights on. He drove the wrong way for two blocks and encountered no one else. He turned onto the first street he knew would take him to the marina. He hoped it was safe to pass there now that the mob had moved downtown.

Within a block, he came to a flank of the demonstration, and people turned on him, throwing rocks and shouting. A few ran after him as he quickly backed up the street again.

Someone shouted, "Look, a rental car! A foreigner. Get him!" The R license plate was a dead giveaway for a rental and, therefore, a foreigner of some kind. The hair on Wilson's neck rose, and a shiver of fear ran through him. He began to panic.

Suddenly fourteen men were running his way with long wooden sticks in their hands, a few with placards, all with hate in their eyes. Wilson reversed as fast as he could on the narrow street. The deep, treacherous storm gutters on each side of the road yawned open, just waiting for him to swerve into them and hang his car up on the chassis. One wheel in there and he would never get out without a tow. But the gutter made it hard for the men chasing him to run alongside him and break the side windows of the car. They seemed content running up close and striking the car's hood with their clubs and sticks. Sweat poured from Wilson's face as he locked eyes with one of the rioters. *That man will kill me if he can,* he thought.

He reversed to the next side street and immediately turned left, driving several blocks farther along the hillside to the next street he knew would take him to safety. The runners fell away as he lurched forward and escaped. As he came out onto the road that ran to Grand Anse, he knew he'd been lucky. There were only a few stragglers left in the area, and a policeman waved him through the main intersection. He was safe. He let out a deep breath and wiped the sweat off his face with his hands. *That was close,* he thought.

Across the harbor, he could see fires where the demonstrators were burning pallets stored along the quay. The demonstration had turned into another riot. He wondered who was behind it. Who would benefit from another violent altercation? If this kept up, many people would be afraid to be on the streets at night.

He drove back to the hotel, and Leslie, the guard, commented on the damaged vehicle. "No insurance gonna pay for riot damage, Mr. Wilson. Best say a tree fell on da car." He chortled.

"Thank you, Leslie. I may do just that." He inspected the hood when he parked the car. Just what he needed. The hood was dented in several places, paint chipped off here and there.

He crept along the vegetation-lined pathway to his room. It was only ten o'clock, and he should have talked to Gordon one more time, but then there was the possibility of a Vargas encounter. Instead, he crept directly to his room.

Something seemed off as he entered his room, and he went on alert immediately. He moved around the room carefully, checking that nothing was missing and that no one was there. Then he examined his computer to be sure it had not been tampered with. It was very secure, so no one could break into his machine without his passwords or a supercomputer to decrypt his accounts. But it looked like it had been moved from the position he had left it in that afternoon. Maybe the maid came in and dusted again. He couldn't be sure, but nothing else seemed out of place.

He let it go but decided he could not leave his computer out in the open from then on. It had been a very long day, so he simply called it a night. He lay there with the patio door open, the sea breeze ruffling the curtains and a light rain pattering on the patio railing. He couldn't sleep.

As he reviewed the day's events, he felt as though he was missing something. He raised himself up on one elbow and stared out to sea. The black freighter seemed to mock him as it rode the waves silently, revealing nothing and yet taunting him with its secrets.

Chapter 7

Friday

The next morning began with a rain shower and a stiff sea wind. The waves on the beach were higher than usual, reducing the number of bathers but providing more challenge to the hardy souls who surfed the breakers. Heavy clouds hung over the island's central mountains, suggesting that late-afternoon rain would fall. Rainstorms often formed on the dark, rain-forested heights and then swept down to the lower elevations. The clouds were an indicator of a downpour to come.

Wilson had breakfast on the hotel patio, where they always delivered a big buffet of fruits, an egg station, baked goods, assorted side dishes, and smoked back bacon, the English equivalent of American bacon. The coffee was fresh Grenada beans roasted to perfection.

He read the local weekly newspaper, the *Bomb*. There was a short article about the damage inflicted downtown by last night's so-called peaceful demonstration that turned ugly. Most damage was against inanimate things; there were only a few injuries to people who were trapped by the mob. All commentary by locals was that this was not like Grenada at all. They never had riots in the street like this, at least not for many years. *So what's changed?* he wondered. Was it just overly enthusiastic campaigning, or did someone organize the riot?

He sat at the table and observed the other guests, mostly vacationers as the weekend approached. There was a small group from Trinidad, a wedding party assembling for the big day, and several tables of Venezuelans, some subdued by hangovers, some just beginning to party again. They seemed to have a lot of time on their hands—no one seemed to be discussing the conference.

Gordon came to the table and told him his friend had arrived, so Wilson signed off on the bill and followed him at a distance to the laundry building. Gordon nodded toward one door and then continued on with his other duties. Wilson looked around to be sure he was not observed.

Wilson turned the door latch and stepped into a laundry sorting room used by the staff for folding and pressing linens, sheets, and towels. He crossed to the other side of the room, where a small, bald black man stood admiring the view out of a ground-level window. He was known to Wilson only as Edgar, one of the people behind the NSP campaign. His position with that group was unclear, but he was pointed out to Wilson as a man who could arrange a street demonstration at the Wong site. He got right to the point.

"Some of my people want to postpone again. The police are really uptight about the riot last night and may not give us a permit for a gathering." He looked grim. "I don't know whether to press the matter or if you can postpone. All I know is this favor may become difficult to provide. Gordon said it was important, so I assume there is a good reason for it."

"It's important to draw attention to the influence that the Chinese have on the island, isn't it?"

"Yes, but in this manner? I wonder if we cannot just do a letter-writing campaign." He hesitated. "And why must it be at night? And so late? It will not gain much television attention."

"I can't be more specific about the reasons behind the demonstration. But it is important." Wilson had a sinking feeling. "How about tomorrow night?"

"In that case, I will see what I can do. I will pass an answer through Gordon." He looked even more grim-faced than before but attempted a smile to show his support. Then he left the room through another doorway after checking that he would not be seen by a passerby.

Wilson stood for a moment in thought. He realized he needed a backup plan. He would talk to Madeline to see if she had any ideas. In any case, they would postpone the operation until Saturday night, another delay.

He left the laundry and walked back to his room via the jungle path he had come to enjoy, with its birdlife and flowers everywhere. The maid was in the room, as evidenced by her service cart outside the door. He knocked and entered, saying, "Good morning," as he did.

"Good morning," she said, smiling as she continued her work.

He picked up his computer and continued to the balcony as she sang to herself and scrubbed the sink in the bathroom. She was a new maid to him. Perhaps because it was Friday, the day for a shift change.

On the balcony, he turned his gaze to the black freighter, which floated exactly where it had been all week. He scanned it with his binos in case there had been any change on board. The position of the rear crane was a little different; perhaps they had shifted one of the containers on the deck for some reason. He could see three men repairing one of the antennas, and they may have installed another revolving radar unit on top of the stern structure, but that was it. Nothing else seemed out of character.

The maid called out that she was finished and left the room with a soft click of the door. He set about reading email messages from Langley. They had another question about the surveillance he had proposed and had passed it up the ranks to the section chief for his approval on Monday. Of course, as far as they knew, it was happening tonight. It wouldn't matter what they eventually decided. It would be too late.

Langley did have information on the container numbers that he had sent them. There was concern that there had been a transmission error because a few of the numbers from the hidden containers did not make sense. They were attributed to units that had been lost at sea on board the *El Faro* freighter during Hurricane Joaquin in October 2015. Because the ship sank with all hands, and all onboard freight was lost, the numbers must be incorrect. He was instructed to verify the numbers in the field and resubmit them for analysis.

He sat back in his chair and pondered the news. Could there have been an error with the numbers of the containers on *El Faro*? That seemed unlikely, as any insurance claims would have led to extensive verification of what had been on board and sunk and what was not. Still, he sent a message asking for verification of the numbers lost on the *El Faro* and said he would verify the numbers on his end.

Another possibility came to mind. Maybe someone had repainted the numbers on the hidden containers so that no one could tell which ship they really came from, just in case someone like Wilson came along and questioned them. It would be an easy enough change and hard to detect unless someone in the harbor noticed a problem with the numbering or paint.

He would need an accounting of all Wong containers offloaded in Saint George's since Wong began its work several months before. Then he might be able to estimate how many units were unaccounted for. He could see if some of them were renumbered as the hidden containers. If he asked Lightchurch to collect this information through his source, they might get a response today, Friday, before the weekend. He sent off a coded message right away.

He finished all communication and locked up his computer in a case he carried with him. He left a message for Madeline and then decided he would look for her at the warehouse. With that in mind, he stepped out of the room and into the outdoor corridor that ran along the length of the building.

To his surprise, he bumped into Tori Vargas.

"So, Roberto, this is where you are hiding out." Vargas was very enthusiastic as usual, a radiant smile on her lips. "I wondered if you were still at the hotel." She put a hand on his arm and leaned into him. "Listen, Roberto. I am so sorry and embarrassed about yesterday. I don't know what happened. I guess I had too much rum."

"Hi, Tori," he said, improvising. "Do you feel OK today?"

"Oh yes." She smiled and then looked frustrated. "I can't remember what happened, except that I woke up on my bed that afternoon still in my bathing suit. I remember us walking to my room, then nothing."

"You passed out, so I helped you into your room. You were dead asleep by that time." He saw a question on her face. "Don't worry. Nothing happened."

Relief flooded her features. "Oh, you are such a gentleman, Roberto. How can I make it up to you?"

He felt trapped, so he took the easy way out. "It would be nice to talk and have a cocktail, but I'm late for a meeting now. Maybe we can talk later? I could call you when I get back to the hotel."

"Oh, let me give you my phone number. Maybe dinner?" She looked hopeful. She fumbled in her purse for a pen. She found one and then looked for a piece of paper. "Here, give me your hand." Before he could pull away, she was writing her number on his palm. "There, now you can't lose it."

He retracted his hand and said goodbye. She stood there as he walked quickly away. He reached the car park and climbed inside his rental. He couldn't believe what was happening. He was a little angry at being caught off guard like that. But he was attracted to the woman too. He would have to make a clean break somehow or things could get even more complicated.

He thought she was just looking for a fling, not anything serious or business related. It was just an instinct that he had. He wouldn't mind that sort of thing himself if he wasn't in the middle of an operation. She seemed like a nice woman to know better, except of course for her employer. It couldn't really work out. But still, he wouldn't just dump her. He liked her.

Rain began to fall on the windshield. That was when he noticed there was a crack in the glass where a stone had hit it last night. He hadn't seen it in the dark. He would deal with it later. He backed the car up and drove out the front gate, nodding to the guard on duty as he went. He had to think. Maybe he could have Gordon tell Vargas that there was a Mrs. Wilson, at least as far as he was aware. Maybe that would work and let her down gently.

***

It rained on and off all afternoon, never becoming intense but enough that you had to carry an umbrella at all times. When he arrived at the warehouse, Madeline was there packing rucksacks. She opened the door, and he rushed in out of the rain.

"It's a no go for tonight," he said immediately. "The people at NSP are getting cold feet after last night's riot. The police won't issue a permit either."

She spun around and stared at him. "Shit, man. That's bad news." She looked disappointed. "We need that diversion."

"We'll have to improvise. Something ordinary. No demonstration. Like a drive-by with Molotov cocktails. But we still need someone to execute the plan."

"Let me tell Lightchurch." She picked up her secure cell phone and moved away to dial a number.

Wilson took the opportunity to visit the men's room, where he washed the ink from his hand after memorizing Vargas's phone number. He might need to call her later. When he exited the bathroom, Madeline was already pacing the floor.

"He said he'll see what he can do to help. I feel like I've let the old man down." Her downcast eyes told that story, a frown on her face.

"Don't worry. We'll think of something." He walked over and put a hand on her shoulder. "But we must decide now if we should postpone until tomorrow."

She straightened up, standing close to him. "We'll have to postpone. He can't get another team together by tonight."

"True." He walked over to the table and leaned against it as he thought. She paced the floor.

"Did you get up there and recon last night to learn the guard schedule?" He remembered her plan to do so.

"Yes, no problem. They generally shut down construction by six o'clock, right at dark. Most people leave the site but some walk to the big warehouse structure in back. Some craftsmen, plumbers, and others who work indoors continue for a couple more hours, then they seem to just camp out in one of the warehouses. The guard shifts are at seven a.m. and seven p.m. sharp. Trucks continue to make deliveries up until about eleven. There are lights in the warehouse until about that time and then everything shuts down, except the guards, of course. They patrol every hour on the half hour on a regular route onsite. They sweep the exterior every two hours on the hour. I made it until three this morning before I cut the cord and came back to my place to sleep."

"Sounds very thorough. Good work." He thought about what she had said. "So we go at two a.m. tomorrow, or technically Sunday morning?"

"Sounds like a plan," she said as she looked at her watch. "Guess we wait and hear from the old man."

There was a crack of thunder outside, and then heavy rain began to drum on the metal roof. "Rain is down," he said. "I hope it rains tomorrow night too."

"What do we do tonight? Besides wait, that is."

"Want to help me see what those Venezuelans are up to out by the airport?" he asked.

"Sure. Sounds like fun."

***

"What did you tell Vargas?" Madeline asked as she and Wilson sat in the front seat of his Noah rental, surveilling the men in the sports facility.

"I said I was stuck up north at Grenville and wouldn't be back until after midnight. She said she would wait up for me."

"That must be hard to turn down." She smiled in a conspiratorial manner at first, then her face hardened to a serious expression. "But remember your cover story. You can't mess around with her during this operation." She poked a finger at him as if he needed a warning. "Be professional and let it go."

"I think I got it covered," he said seriously. "Gordon, the guy at the bar, is going to tell her I'm married. That should cool her jets."

"Kinda mean if you ask me. You should just tell her you're not interested. You're a dedicated family man or some shit like that."

"Right." He sat forward in his seat and pulled his binos up to watch the men at the door of the building where the Venezuelans were. "Hey. What are these guys doing?"

They had been surveilling the address for four hours to get a feel for what the Venezuelans were up to at the rental property. They had sat in the car at two locations where they would be unobtrusive. Then they had split up and spied on the building from different locations on the low hill nearby. They came back to a parked observation point and compared notes. By that time, they were both wet from the intermittent rain showers.

"What we've seen is a lookout front and back, men coming and going. Most are coming and staying inside. I think they might be sleeping in there tonight." Wilson summarized their findings.

"Let's go eat dinner and come back after midnight. That gives us three hours to kill," she said.

"We don't need much for a recon at night, but one weapon might still come in handy in case we're seen," Wilson said.

"Shall we eat at the Boat House at the marina?" Madeline asked. "We can pick up what we need on the way back. I know the restaurant because I live near there."

"Sure, sounds good. You live on a boat or something?"

"No, an apartment just up the hill."

"And I can stop at the hotel for a few things."

"OK, but let's drive now so we have plenty of time," she said.

Finally, they would make a move.

Chapter 8

Saturday

They came back to their parking spot at 12:33 a.m. They were dressed in the same dark clothing they would wear the following night at the construction site. It was a good test of their gear, and the rain was just heavy enough to cover their movements in the dark.

They approached through the parking lot where fifteen Toyota Land Cruisers were lined up along the side of the building. There were guards at the front and back doors, where the two main entrances were located. There were other doors, but they were apparently sealed for unknown reasons. There were five windows along each side of the building, but they had been covered over with cloth curtains on the inside and wooden planking on the exterior, almost like they were shut up for a hurricane. They chose the west side of the building for their approach because there was less light on that side and that was where the vehicles were arrayed.

Wilson went first, scuttling along on his hands and knees between vehicles toward the wall. He reached the first window and evaluated it for a look inside. No luck there. He advanced quietly to the second window while Madeline acted as lookout for any troublesome guards. The second window was also sealed up tight.

At the third window, they had some luck. Apparently someone had pulled back the cloth covering and pushed out one of the planks that was nailed over the window. Cigarette ashes and butts lay on the ground below the window, confirming that several men smoked without leaving the confines of the building.

Thirty or forty butts suggested that many people knew of the open window.

Wilson stood partway up and looked through the narrow gap of the curtain. He could see that there were some low lights on inside, probably so that men could get up to use the restroom facilities during the night. He could see what looked like a series of low platforms arranged in rows on the floor inside. They seemed heaped with something on their tops, making their form hard to identify in the dim light. There were ranks and ranks of them.

Just then Madeline came on the radio earpiece. "Movement by the rear. Stay low."

Wilson looked along the wall and caught sight of a man in uniform rounding the corner of the building, lazily looking up at the sky as he shuffled along the wall. He stopped and faced the wall, fumbling with his pants. It was clear what he was doing, the sound of a trickle of liquid splashing on the ground. Then he began whistling as he pulled up his zipper and returned around the corner to the rear of the building.

As Wilson rose up to the window again, he smelled cigarette smoke and saw a trail of smoky breath billow through the window gap. Someone was standing inside the window having a final smoke. He waited for five minutes. The smoke stopped and shortly thereafter a butt flew out the window.

He returned to the gap and looked inside. This time it was lighter because the door to an inner room was open and its light cast across the entire main area. He could make out that the low rectangular objects were in fact cots with men sleeping on them. There was a stack of equipment along the far wall of the room, long wooden boxes painted drab green.

Another man came toward the window, stopping just before it to light a cigarette. Wilson could see his face clearly in the flickering light of the flame. He was one of the Venezuelans he had seen before at the Hempstead bar. He was too preoccupied to notice Wilson outside.

That was enough. Wilson dropped back to the line of vehicles and crawled over to Madeline. He whispered, "I've seen enough. You want to look?"

"Yes, and maybe I can get a low-light photo too." She crawled up to the window, moving like a black panther through the light rain, her sleek body a shadow against the building wall. She waited for the smoker to finish. Then she cautiously rose up and peered inside. She spent a few minutes taking photos and then returned to Wilson. They both scurried away in the darkness and returned to their parked car.

The rain became torrential as they drove back to the warehouse. They ran through the rain to enter the building. They downloaded and examined the photos on Madeline's laptop. She said, "The lighting was poor, but you can see the beds clearly. It looks like there are ten rows with eight or ten cots per row. That's eighty to one hundred men sleeping there."

"That's a lot of manpower. And they have nothing to do with the conference, as far as I can tell." Wilson clicked through a few more photos, then stopped on one that showed a man standing by an inner doorway. The light partially illuminated his face. "See if you can enhance this guy's face. He might be the one I saw by the window."

Madeline pulled the machine closer to her on the table and opened her copy of Adobe Photoshop. She opened the file and began manipulating it. After five minutes she said, "That's as clear as I can make it with these tools. Do you recognize him?"

Wilson studied the face a few moments. "It's definitely the man who came to the window for a smoke, and I think I've seen him at the hotel bar. He had several men with him on a drinking binge. It seemed like he was in charge."

"OK," she said. "I can have someone with real talent enhance these photos and we may make out other faces then." She paused. "It might be hard to find a technician on the weekend."

"What are they doing with a hundred men hidden near the airport?"

"And those boxes along the back wall looked like shipping crates for rifles. At least the ones I had in view." She sat back in her chair. "They're definitely planning something."

"But what?" He looked over at Madeline's pensive face. "Why there? Why now?"

Madeline stood up and started changing out of her black field clothes, her back to him. He watched her undress and then slip on her street clothes, including flip-flops. She looked over her shoulder at him. "You changin' here?"

He stood up and followed suit, watching her slender form. "Are you a runner? How do you keep fit?"

"Yeah, I run. And swim." She sat on a chair and watched him pull on his clothes. "I never got into weight training, but I do a little to firm up here and there. How about you?"

"More or less the same, but I don't care for indoor pools much. Too much chlorine."

"Get some swimming in while you're here. Best beaches in the world." A wide grin spread across her face. "Maybe we can do a beach day together when this mission is done."

"Sounds good." He grinned at the thought. "Hey, I want to leave my computer here overnight. Do you have a secure room?" He showed her the computer case he had with him.

"Yeah, over here." She walked to a heavy steel door and opened it, revealing equipment inside. "You might keep your gun on you given what we saw tonight. You may need it. I always carry mine." She closed the door and locked it.

"Who's covering Lightchurch while you're with me?"

"He has two regular security men now while I'm on assignment with you. I'll probably go back as his detail when this is all finished." She picked up her day bag and led him out the door to the parking lot.

"We're on schedule for tonight, right?" he said.

"Yes. I'll get the photos reworked and update Lightchurch. What do you have on your plate today?"

"I'll find out more about the Venezuelans and what they're up to. I have to work an asset." He grinned at her and she snickered.

Chapter 9

Saturday

"Thank you for inviting me to lunch today, Roberto," Tori Vargas said warmly. "I had nothing really planned for Saturday and what little I did only took a few hours. So now I am all yours."

She wore very tight shorts that showed off her legs and a shear blouse that revealed her curves at every move. Wilson wondered if she dressed so provocatively all the time. He appreciated her looks and enjoyed her conversation but still wondered if she had an agenda. He certainly did. He must find out if she knew what was happening at the sports facility. If not, he could move on to other sources in his search for information.

"I'm happy you could make lunch. How was the salad? It looked very good."

She smiled sheepishly. "Oh, it was delicious. And the rum punch here is very good." She laughed quietly. "I will have to be more cautious this time and not drink so much like before. I was so embarrassed."

"I already told Gordon that two drinks is your limit—at least during lunch." Wilson was being very pleasant, even doting on her. "But before we become more familiar, I have something I should tell you."

She gave him a serious look, eyes peering into his as if she were plumbing their depths. "Roberto, I know. Gordon was so kind as to tell me. You are still married. Is that what you wished to say?"

"Yes, but I didn't know how to bring it up without being presumptuous." He tried looking innocent. "I wasn't sure you thought of me in that way."

"My friend, we all have our little secrets, don't we?" She gave him a sly grin. "A small affair is not so much, is it?"

"Are you married, Tori?" he asked in an understated voice.

"No, not now. But I once had a man. He was killed three years ago." She looked genuinely sad at the thought. "But not now. I am alone." She attempted a smile.

He smiled and raised his drink for a toast. "Then let's not worry about anything and enjoy our time together, shall we?"

She perked up joyfully. "Yes, let's have some fun. What are the words from that song? *Girls just want to have fun*, yes?" She slurped down some of her punch and looked absolutely carefree.

"Why don't we go swimming before the sun gets too hot?" he suggested. "Then we can relax for the rest of the day, until dinner . . . if you don't have any plans."

Vargas giggled with pleasure at this. "Oh yes. I can try out my swimsuit. It is brand new." She grabbed his hand and stood up beside the table. "Oh, this will be a fun day, yes?" She leaned into him as he stood up and hugged him quickly.

"Great. I'll sign for the bill while you change. Let's meet by the beach gate when you're ready." She hurried off, a large handbag over one shoulder.

Wilson hoped he wasn't getting in over his head. He had the afternoon free to spend with her. If she had some information, he would at least learn some of what she knew. He had a plan. It didn't seem fair, but that was what he had to do.

She was at the beach gate when he returned, and they locked arms as they walked along the sand looking for the ideal spot for their beach chairs. He pulled out two chairs for them and placed them under a small sea grape tree and they spread out their towels. He unbuttoned his shirt and kicked off his shoes. Meanwhile, she dramatically let her cover-up slip off her shoulders, her breasts, and her hips in a breathtaking show of her curved and toned body. She looked like a swimsuit model in her new bikini that covered only a fraction of her breasts, held on by a miracle of design, and the thinnest of strings for her thong.

He dropped his sun hat, stunned. "Wow!" was all he said, which thrilled her. "That is a lovely bikini, Tori. You look fabulous."

She blushed and arranged her towel before doing a full-body stretch that arched her back and drew the attention of everyone for a hundred yards. Even the beach dog came over to check her out, although for different reasons than the men on the sand. The man who rented chairs offered her a chair, even though she sat on one, a beach vendor tried selling her a cover-up, even though she already had one, and a young boy came over and just stared at her boobs. It took a while for the spectacle to lose its fascination so that they could relax.

"That is what happens a lot," she said. "Men just see my body and don't even try talking sometimes."

"So I noticed. There was a man at the bar who was staring at you. I think he might be with the conference."

"What did he look like?" She seemed curious.

"He was tall with black hair and a mustache. He looked like a military type. He had hard black eyes." Wilson described the man he had seen smoking at the window the night before.

Vargas looked at him and then quickly looked away, like she was hiding something. "Oh, him." She stared at the sea and said nothing.

"Is he important? Someone with the conference?"

"No. He is just a man. He is in charge of our security and is very demanding. I don't like working with him."

They sat in the sun for a while, turning over frequently. Wilson had the pleasure of applying sunblock to Vargas's back and shoulders, which elicited a low purr. They ran into the sea and swam for a half hour just to get out of the heat. Finally, after two hours of fun in the sun, they retreated to her hotel room.

They made love for a half hour and then rested under the sheet with the air-conditioning on. They had finished with small talk by then and were ready for round two. She had consumed another rum punch and was quite tipsy. She chattered happily but got a little dreamy now and then. She giggled and moaned when he touched her just right. Afterward, he lay on his back with her nestled into his side and his arm around her.

"I wanted to ask you more about the men here for the conference," he said. "You told me that there were only about seventy people here for the conference, fifteen here in this hotel and about fifty at the other hotel. What's it called?"

"The Best Beach Hotel, I think."

"And how about the men at the sports facility by the airport? Why are they here?" He asked this casually and watched her face for a response.

"Oh, how do you know . . . ?" She turned her face toward him, searching for a response.

"You told me the other day when we were drinking. Don't you remember?" He downplayed it as much as possible. "How many are over there?"

She didn't say anything at first, except, "I did?" Her face was puzzled. "I don't remember." She seemed to struggle with her memory and what she should say.

"Are they all military men? Is the man who was at the bar one of them?"

Her features showed distress. She got up on one elbow and looked into his face. "How do you know this? Did I tell you?"

Then a trace of fear crossed her brow. "*Dios mio*. Maybe I did. I have what you call blackouts sometimes."

"Blackouts from drinking?"

"Yes, but what did I do? Did I really tell you about them? I could get in trouble for this." She settled into his shoulder again for a minute or two while he stroked her arm with his fingers. "I do not know what the men are doing. It is for security. All I know is that one hundred men are staying somewhere else until the election is over. They will join with many of our people at the other hotel and work together on something. That is all they told me." She stopped and rose on her elbow to look into his eyes. "Do not tell anyone or I can get in trouble."

"Why? Who would you get in trouble with?" He wanted to let her tell him her woes—slowly.

"That man at the bar is my boss here. He is mean to me. He is head of security." She lay back down again with her head on his shoulder.

"What's his name? Is he in the military?"

"He is Major Cortez. He is in charge of everything. He could punish me." She looked up at him with fear in her eyes. "Did I really tell you? Oh, I am in trouble." She looked away, her anguish etched on her features.

He tried being helpful and pulled her to him. "Don't be afraid. I won't tell anyone. It's just you and me, OK?"

They lay there in silence for nearly three minutes. He rubbed her shoulder, and they kissed gently a few times. He told her how beautiful she was. Her face began to relax, and she turned back to him, her eyes hopeful.

"Can I trust you, Roberto?"

"Yes, Tori. We are lovers. We can share anything."

"Well, I have a secret. Can I tell you?"

"Yes. What is so secret?"

"I hate my job," she said firmly. She rose onto one elbow again, looking sideways at him. "I have a terrible job."

"Why is it so terrible? You get to travel to nice places like this."

"Yes, once a year, maybe more if you count going to Cuba. It is not so nice there. Not where we stay." She seemed to relax as she spoke. "At first it was exciting, three years ago when I started. There was more money then and we could do things, go places. And I was just one of the women who arranged travel."

"Then what happened?"

"My husband worked for the same department but in a different office. He was arrested for stealing papers." Her voice broke and she was silent. "I don't know what he did. He said he did nothing, but they did not believe him. He went to jail." She stopped again and breathed deeply several times. "They threatened me into testifying against him, but I said I knew nothing about it. It was very bad."

Wilson listened and wondered if this was a cover story she had prepared to gain his sympathy. It sounded plausible, and she seemed like she was speaking from the heart.

"Then what happened?"

"We had been getting help for my parents because of our jobs. My mother has a bad—what is the gland in your throat that regulates everything in the body?"

"The thyroid?"

"Yes, maybe the thyroid gland. She needed medicine every day or she would get very ill and die. So the government gave us the medicine for our work. It was OK." She became silent again.

"What happened?"

"When he was arrested, they said they would not do this for my mother anymore. They did not care about her. They would do it only if I testified against my husband. Do you understand?"

"I think I'm starting to. Did you testify?" He placed his face beside hers and saw the deep pain she felt.

She began to cry on his shoulder and he comforted her. She shuddered for a minute and then seemed to calm down. Her face was wet from tears running down her checks, her mascara ruined. He handed her a tissue, and she wiped away the tears.

"Yes, I did. But I said only that I did not know what he did. Somehow—I don't know how—they turned what I said into evidence against him." Tears ran down her cheeks again. "And then he was hanged in prison." She sobbed loudly then—big, heartbreaking sobs that spoke of her misery and guilt.

She cried openly, spilling an ocean of tears onto his chest. She sobbed for a long time. He waited quietly. This is not what he had hoped to achieve. He felt he was using her badly.

"They buried him in a mass grave, so I can't even go to his grave and beg for forgiveness. It is terrible."

"It's not your fault, Tori. You wanted to help him and your parents too. You had no choice."

"But then my boss told me I had to do more for my job in order to keep the medicine for my mother. They told me I must do things. Bad things. To help the state. To help my country." She stopped sobbing and turned to look at his face. "They said I could use my beauty to help the government." She was sniffling now, having run out of tears.

"What did they make you do?"

"I arranged things to make men happy. Find them girls for sex. Get them whiskey and drugs if they wanted them. And for important men, provide the sex myself." She looked up at him again. "I don't like it, Roberto. Do not think too badly of me. I'm not a whore." Her eyes showed complete devastation.

He thought about what she had said. She was confessing everything to him. Why? Was it a trap? Or was it real? He felt sorry for her.

"And you were supposed to sleep with me? Or is this real? Because you like me?"

She sat up with her legs crossed and faced him on the bed. She stroked her left breast with her fingers. "They told me you were an important journalist and I should get you to notice me. It is not so hard. Men always stare at my body, my face, my tits, my ass. I know it is only natural, but my trainer said I can learn to use this to make men talk about their work, to get their secrets." She stopped.

"And then what?"

"Well, I watched you to see what you were like. Major Cortez said I should find a way to sleep with you. Make you fall in love with me so that he could learn what you are doing here. He suspects you are not really a journalist." She looked at Wilson in a strange way, her eyes searching his face for something.

"But I am a writer and journalist. I don't work for any one newspaper like most reporters; I do historical writing. Maybe that looked suspicious to Cortez." Wilson wondered what she was getting at.

She got on her hands and knees and crawled over Wilson so that she could lie on top of him, their chests rubbing together, their faces inches apart. She stared at him and they kissed. Her eyes brightened.

"Roberto, he thinks you are a spy." She smiled wanly then. Her eyes were locked on his. She stared right into him and smiled as if she had discovered something. Then she kissed him warmly on the lips.

"I knew it." She kissed him again. He could not help but kiss her, too, long wet, warm, telling kisses.

"But I am not a spy, Tori. Just a writer."

"No, I see it now. And he cannot be wrong. He is with the Cuban intelligence service. They make no mistakes."

Wilson was shocked. How had they made him? And Cortez was a Cuban agent? Why didn't Langley warn him? Now he thought back to the files he had read about this operation. Somewhere they had mentioned Cuban involvement but not at this level of operation.

She made love to him, making it difficult for him to think clearly as his body responded. She straddled him and rode him slowly. He couldn't help himself. Then she talked to him in a quiet voice.

"Now we must finish with a good performance and show I am working," she whispered. "I will make it last so we can talk. There is a camera in the room but no sound, I think."

"What?" he asked breathlessly. "Where is it?"

"I won't tell you or you will look right at it and they will know I told you. And don't look around. Just enjoy the sex and listen." She rode him harder, getting his attention, then slowed down again. "I am telling you this because I want out of Venezuela. I want you to get my parents out and then me out too. Do you understand?" Her voice was a whisper, and her face implored him for help.

He nodded. She leaned down and kissed him. It was a warm kiss, and he enjoyed it immensely. He felt ready to explode. How had this happened? How was he supposed to respond? Then he came in a rush. She seemed to come too. Or was she acting? She crashed down on top of him.

"I will do whatever you want," she whispered in his ear. "I can get some information and take it with me. I can give you names, lots of names. I can tell you about Cortez and my boss and the crimes they have committed. Cortez leads the secret police squads that make people disappear at night. He likes to burn people for torture. He is in the *Servicio Bolivariano de Inteligencia Nacional*, the SEBIN. You know of their work. I can bring you this."

"Why me?" he asked softly as he rubbed his face against hers. "Why tell me all this?"

"Because they plan to kill you if you are a spy." She pulled away a few inches; her eyes told him it was true. "You must help me now and I will help you. I must show them that you are not a spy. How to do this?"

"I'm not a spy. You must tell them that."

"If I don't have proof, they will think I lied. That would be bad for us both, Roberto." Her face was against his, her lips warm on his lips.

"OK, I believe you. But I must think. I must go and find a way." He kissed her. "I had better go and get a plan together. We can meet again tomorrow afternoon. By then I will have something you can show them."

"Good, Roberto, but no later. I see Cortez for a meeting in the morning." Her voice broke and tears rolled down her cheeks. "He always fucks me rough during the meeting. But I can tell him we have a date tomorrow night. You can give me something then."

They dressed slowly and kissed goodbye at the door. He left, his mind numb after their conversation. She stayed in the room looking grim. Wilson's head was cluttered with thoughts about this new challenge. He had to sort this situation out. He had a chance to gain information from inside the Venezuelan intelligence service and to develop a mole in their organization, at least for a short while. But how to get them off his tail? Tori Vargas presented both a potential asset and a liability. Which would she become?

Chapter 10

Sunday

Wilson and Madeline were creeping quietly through the soggy forest just up slope of the Wong Construction site at 1:45 a.m. It was pitch black and raining heavily. The moon was completely shrouded in black clouds. Lightning was the only natural light, causing everything to appear frozen in motion in the strobe-like illumination. They wore headlamps that projected a weak reddish hue onto the vegetation directly in front of them, enough light to see the trail but not bright enough to make out details or to be seen from any distance.

They were humping along the trail that Wilson had covered three days before and getting soaked from the constant contact with wet vegetation. Neither of them spoke out loud, although they both muttered under their breath about the quality of the wet conditions and the slippery ground. They turned off the trail and headed downhill toward the back fence of the construction site. He led the way because he had been here before, but, quite frankly, he couldn't recognize anything in the rain. They both took turns falling when their feet skidded out from under them. The heavy packs and the awkward size of the bolt cutters made for an unpleasant stroll.

They came upon the fence quicker than expected, testing it to be sure it wasn't electrified in some way. In the rain, that would have made their mission impossible. They both looked carefully all around the fence for booby traps as well as for any signs of guards or dogs that could surprise them. Then Wilson pulled the bolt cutters from his pack and began cutting through the fence one link at a time. The cutters did their job well, but it took time in the rain.

Then they backed away from the fence into the soaking bushes and waited.

At twenty seconds past two o'clock, they heard the first boom. Bang! Whoosh! Then another and another, all coming from the front of the property. Then they heard automatic weapons fire and the hiss of a fire burning out of control. Voices shouted, guns fired, car engines roared, and it sounded as though twenty Chinese men were yelling in pandemonium down along the fence by Morne Rouge Road.

There was noise from the warehouse just east of them in the forest. A metal door crashed open and three men ran outside, just a hundred yards from Wilson and Madeline. The two burglars waited for a few seconds, ensuring that no one came their way. Fortunately, the three men ran toward the front of the property, shouting in Chinese. When it was clear that no one else would head in their direction, Wilson stepped through the hole they had made in the fence, followed by Madeline. They hustled over to the closest of the hidden containers.

Madeline clamped the jaws of the bolt cutter onto the first padlock, and it snapped in two easily. The second one took all their combined might to cut the lock, but it yielded as well. They swung open the left door and looked inside.

The container was packed to the roof with pallets of green wooden boxes. Identification numbers were printed on each box, and many of them appeared to be part of a series of IDs.

"These are rifle shipping crates. Let's open one up," Madeline whispered.

Wilson pulled out a pry bar and worked on a box that was close at hand. Madeline helped rip the cover off it and then they both looked at each other. Inside each box were ten rifles. He pulled one out and examined it. "AK-74, the newer version of the AK-47. There are at least thirty boxes in here."

Madeline took low-light photos of the open box, a close-up of the rifle, and a shot of the interior of the container, showing how many boxes were inside. Then they stepped out of the container and closed the door. She took a photo of the container that showed its ID number.

They moved on to the next container and cut the locks off it. Inside were dozens of smaller green wooden boxes covered with numbers. They cracked one open and found it packed with ammunition for the AKs next door. They documented their find.

"Holy shit, Maddie. They must have a hundred thousand rounds of ammo in there."

They opened the next container and found more ammo. Another container had more of the same type of rifles. A fifth had boxes of grenades and belts of ammunition for machine guns. Another had RPG rockets and firing tubes inside. They documented everything they saw with photos. They threw the cut padlocks inside each container so as not to draw attention to the unlocked doors.

Madeline grabbed Wilson's arm and pointed toward her wristwatch. They were out of time and should retreat. She put her hand to her ear and pointed toward the front of the property. There were three loud explosions. Bang! Whoosh! All were about ten seconds apart and then they heard rifle fire and loud shouting in Chinese. Several men ran out of the warehouse again, shouting and, in one case, waving a rifle in the air. This time they left the large garage-like door open and light flooded out onto the vegetation behind the building.

"Let's try to look inside," Wilson said, shifting in that direction in a crouch.

Madeline spoke quietly over her lip mic. "Not in the plan. Not a good idea, Robert." Her voice was strained.

But he was already halfway to the rear of the warehouse, and she had no choice but to follow, staying low in the shadows. They cut uphill into the shrubs when they got closer to the lighted doorway. Then they crept through the bushes slowly and quietly until they were lined up with the doorway and could see inside.

Inside the warehouse, they saw at least twenty two-ton trucks decorated in a camo green pattern, with Grenada Defense Force lettering on them. The problem was that Grenada did not have a defense force. The trucks were loaded with equipment and green boxes similar to those they had seen in the containers. Many men wearing drab green uniforms stood around tables, and they could see hammocks suspended along the walls of the huge room. Then they saw what looked like a series of portable rocket launchers mounted on trailers and four radar stations on trucks. Madeline set about recording everything they saw on low-light video. "This is weird shit, Robert," she whispered.

The sounds of chaos at the front of the property stopped, and only limited noises reached their ears. They heard a fire truck rushing up the road from the Grand Anse Fire Station and then men shouting in English about the fires. That was when several men came back to the warehouse from the front of the property.

The men walked around the corner of the building, and most walked inside. Three men, including the one with the rifle, shouted back and forth in Mandarin and started walking toward the bushes where Wilson and Madeline were hiding. Their purpose became clear when each man reached for the zipper on his pants and they stepped up to the edge of the bushes. The two burglars froze in place. *This is bad news*, Wilson thought. *We gotta get out of here.*

There was a lot of discussion about something funny in Mandarin as they peed. When done, they zipped up and were backing away when one of them dropped something in the grass near the shrubs. The man bent down to pick it up and came eye to eye with Madeline. She was greased up with face camo paint and did not move a muscle, but the man stopped dead and screamed as he tripped back away from the bushes, landing on his back in the wet grass.

He shouted that he had seen something, but the other men just laughed at him. One patted him on the back and made a big joke out of it. But the frightened man argued that they do something; it wasn't clear what. Then he suddenly grabbed the rifle away from the man who had it and fired several rounds into the bushes. That caused the other men to shout and then laugh at his antics. Finally, another man, apparently more senior, ran out of the building and asked what they were shooting at. He jerked the rifle away from the frightened man and began giving him a lecture as he swatted his face with an open hand. They all walked back into the warehouse.

When they were inside, Wilson began creeping through the bushes to their left and away from the warehouse. He realized that he had been holding his breath the whole time. Now he breathed out and said softly into his lip mic, "That was too damn close."

Madeline whispered, "More than close. I was hit."

"What?" He stopped in his tracks and spun around. "Where?"

"I got nicked in the side. Not too bad, I think, but it hurts like hell."

"Let's see. Show me," he said.

"Not here. I can wait a couple of minutes until we get out of the fence."

"You sure?"

"Yeah. Let's move." She took the lead, walking carefully.

They climbed through the hole in the fence and then used light steel wire to reclose it in a crude manner. They couldn't leave an obvious trail that they had come that way.

As they started humping their packs through the forest, Madeline whispered, "OK. Here."

She pointed to her left arm, where blood was seeping through her shirtsleeve. "I got hit by that idiot with the AK. I got to wrap it up or I'll leave a blood trail."

"Shit, Maddie." He reached for her arm. "Where is it? The blood's on the inside of your arm."

"It's my chest under the arm. I think it nicked a rib too. It hurts like hell."

He tore open the side of her shirt and saw the wound. "It's not deep. I'll put a gauze pad there, and it will stem the bleeding awhile. We have to get out of here." He dropped his pack and searched for his first aid kit. He found the gauze pads and tore open the packaging on three of them, giving them to her so that she could pack them against the wound. She winced. He picked up the paper wrappers so that there would be no trace of their passing. Then, as she held her breath, he secured tape over the gauze to keep it in place.

"How's that?" he asked as she gripped his arm.

"It's OK," she said through clenched teeth. "I can make it."

He threw on his rucksack and grabbed hers. They staggered away into the night.

***

"I think the bleeding has stopped," she said. "But it still hurts like hell."

They had made it to Madeline's apartment, where Wilson had hidden the car in back behind some bushes. He had helped her upstairs and dropped the packs on the floor. He came back from the bathroom with a hand towel soaked in warm water.

"Here, let's get your shirt off and see what we got." She sat up on the side of the bed and tried pulling the tight-fitting and rain-soaked shirt off her back. She struggled and cried out in pain. "Shit, I can't get it."

He pulled out his folding knife and cut the shirt so that she could shed it more easily. She winced with pain. "What's it look like? I can't see."

"Not too bad. I'll cut away your bra to get at it."

"Like hell. This is a twenty-dollar black bra. They're hard to get in Grenada." She held her breath as she reached around and unclasped it so that it fell away. Then she turned sideways and looked under her armpit at the injury. She lay on her side at the edge of the bed so that he could work on the wound.

Wilson felt like hell, believing himself responsible for her injury. If he hadn't rushed over to look in the warehouse, she wouldn't have been shot. It was as simple as that. It was his fault.

He removed the blood-soaked gauze pads and gently washed the wound with the towel while she bit into a sheet for the pain. He examined it carefully. The bleeding was minimal now. He washed it twice, getting more water from the sink.

"It's a flesh wound but a little deep. It hit the bone here." He pressed on one spot.

"Watch it! That hurts like hell," she moaned.

"The bullet tore your skin coming in and laid back part of the muscle as it passed through. I have to fold the skin back down and tape it up. I'll put on antibiotic and a painkiller too." He opened a pack of blood astringent and poured it on the worst part of the wound. Then he applied the disinfectant from the gunshot kit and carefully closed up the skin. He taped it over with butterfly bandages.

"That's as good as I can do now, Maddie." He got up and asked her if she could sit up. She struggled but rose upright on the side of the bed.

"Oh fuck! That hurts," she said. She tried to straighten up, then appeared self-conscious because her dark breasts were bare. She put one arm across her breasts to cover them.

"Give me some rum to drink, will you? It will help." He looked away from her while he poured two stiff glasses of Westerhall light rum, neat, into two old-fashioned glasses. She took a glass in one hand while holding her other arm across her chest.

"Here's to a successful mission," she said and downed the rum. She smiled weakly. "Ow. Jesus, that stings."

"We better call in and let Lightchurch know where we are." He handed her cell phone to her.

"No, you call. See if we have a doctor available who can be discreet." She tried lying down on the bed but winced again. She sipped the rum, feeling miserable.

"Let me call first, then I'll help you lie down." He stepped into her small kitchen and dialed in. They talked for three minutes. "There's a doctor we could use, but he's not in Saint George's tonight. We'll get you in to see him first thing tomorrow."

"In that case, help me get these wet pants off so I can sleep." She had them unbuttoned but only halfway down her legs. He carefully pulled them off, leaving her with only her panties on. She slipped into a light cotton kimono that she retrieved from the closet. She scooted back on the bed as he pulled the bedsheet out of her way. She moved to the far side of the bed, sitting up against the headboard.

"Don't take this as an invitation, but I don't have a couch for you to sleep on."

"I can sleep on the floor," he suggested. "Or go back to the hotel."

"Don't be crazy. Sleep on the bed, but that's all, OK?"

He poured them both more rum and turned off the overhead light, leaving only the lamp in the kitchen illuminated. He pulled off his wet clothes and hung them on the back of a chair. Then he slid in under the sheet beside her.

"You want to talk about the mission or just sleep?" he asked.

"Sleep." She finished her drink and set the glass on the nightstand on her side of the bed.

He got up and turned off the lamp in the kitchen, then slid under the sheet again. She turned toward him and put her head on the pillow beside his, her body positioned with her wounded side up.

"I can sleep on this side. Is this OK?" she whispered, her face inches from his. She closed her eyes.

She fell asleep almost immediately. He lay on his back listening to her breathe. He soon fell into a dream in which he and Madeline relived their stealthy exploit through the stormy forest in the dark. It seemed surreal. Then men in green uniforms were chasing them. It went on and on.

Chapter 11

Sunday

Wilson, Madeline, and Lightchurch were gathered inside the operation warehouse, evaluating what they had learned during the previous night's activities. Heavy rain poured down outside and drummed loudly on the metal roof of the structure. During the night, there had been some street flooding, and a storm was whipping up the sea into six-foot waves. The waves rushed up the beach as far at the vegetation line and some seawalls. It was not a severe storm yet, but there was concern that there could be mass flooding of low-lying areas along the coast.

"I have to tell you it was quite exciting last night, driving like mad while Nash threw out those Molotov bombs." Lightchurch laughed as he recounted the tale, standing next to the worktable. "We caught them completely off guard on the first pass, but on the second they landed a few rounds on the truck. Lucky Nash wasn't hit."

"You were damn lucky, I'd say." Madeline chastised the old man for his actions. "You said you had a team to carry out the diversion, not that you would be there yourself. That is damn reckless of you."

"Good thing you had Nash there," Wilson said. "At least *he* knew what he was doing."

"Now don't you come down on me too, Robert. I haven't had so much fun in I don't know how long." He smiled from ear to ear. "But you're right. Nash stole the truck for us and ditched it afterward. Imagine what the police are going to think when they find it. I can see the headline in the newspaper now: 'Island

Radicals Attack Chinese Workforce.' Just imagine the trouble it will cause. Maybe now they'll crack down on these riots we're having."

"I heard on the radio this morning that it was a protest against foreigners in the country," Wilson said. "Since the GPC is pro-China, the reporter assumed that the NSP was behind it somehow." He walked to where Madeline was working on her computer. "How are you feeling?" he asked. "Has the anesthetic worn off yet?"

"It's starting to hurt again." She shifted around in her chair, uncomfortable in a loose-fitting pullover and shorts. "The doc said I can get back to normal work in four weeks. He sewed up the muscle and said that I can't tear it again, so that's my weak spot right now." She grimaced whenever she twisted her body.

"Well, it could have been a lot worse." He put a hand on her shoulder. "I'm sorry. I shouldn't have gone and checked out the warehouse like that without a plan. I got you hurt."

She turned partway around, groaned, and smiled at him. "It's a good thing we got a look inside that building. Here's the video I shot from the bushes." She pointed to the computer screen. "It turned out pretty well considering the bad lighting and rain."

"What you two found last night is very disturbing to me," Lightchurch said calmly. "It looks like someone is planning military action in the near future, perhaps during the election."

"I'm sorry the still photos came out so ambiguously, Sir," Madeline said softly. "You can still make out the boxes and some of the lettering. I guess the lens of that camera had a poor seal on it and moisture steamed it up."

"Don't worry, Maddie." Lightchurch looked her in the eye. "Really, you two got enough to show our friends that something unusual is going on. That's what matters." He paused and put a hand on her shoulder. "But you were both lucky to not get caught. And I, of course, wish you had gotten away unscathed."

"The Chinese are involved," Wilson said as he paced the floor. "That much hardware and ammo can only mean a coup is being planned." He stopped and pointed at the computer screen. "We saw enough arms for at least two companies of men. And I'd like to know why they have what look like surface-to-air missiles."

"It is troubling," Lightchurch agreed. "I need to think about what we do next with this information." He paused and then looked up expectantly. "But what do you make of the container numbering problem, Robert? Have you worked out more there?"

Wilson was surprised by the sudden change in topics. "Yes. I've accounted for all forty-foot containers that have come in on ships to the harbor." He stopped speaking as he gathered his thoughts. "But there is still a discrepancy, even when I account for the fact that some have been renumbered." He stepped to the table where he pulled a sheet of paper from his briefcase. "According to the harbor logs, one hundred fifty-six containers were unloaded from ships for Wong Construction projects in the last twelve months. Twenty-two of those containers were later shipped out, leaving one hundred thirty-four containers still on the island. On Wednesday, there were sixty-three containers in the main work area, some open, some closed. At the back of the property, there were an additional forty-eight containers that I refer to as the hidden containers. That makes twenty-three containers more than there should be. Those are the ones with uncertain numbers on them." He began pacing again.

"Twenty-three extras? How's that even possible?" Lightchurch exclaimed, sitting down on a chair at the table.

"I don't know, but there must be twenty-three missing containers somewhere else. They didn't just appear out of nowhere," Madeline commented. "We'll need more help from the harbor master on this. Can you arrange that, Sir?"

"Yes. I'll call over there now."

Wilson's phone pinged. "I have an email from Langley. Let me check it out." He walked to the table where his laptop was located. Indeed, he had received a message he had been waiting for; it was a collection of articles he had written at one time or another for the *Miami Observer* and two articles about Jamaican elections and their effect on the economy within two years of the event.

"Hey, I got the material I need for Tori Vargas. I can give it to her today when I see her."

Madeline looked up from her computer and snickered. "You mean when you boff her, don't you?" She emitted a hard laugh that made Lightchurch cringe.

Wilson gave her a disappointed look. "It's not my idea. I'm her assignment, so give me a break, will you?" He shook a finger at Madeline, who shook a finger back in a menacing way. "But I must find a way to talk to her without being heard. I'd take her to my room, but that may have been bugged by now too. Which reminds me—I should move out of there."

Madeline spun around and then winced from the motion. "You can't move. If you do, they'll know you're on to them. It would compromise her too. And this time Romeo and Juliette will be on camera with sound." She laughed again and covered her mouth when Lightchurch gave her a dirty look. "I wonder if I can get a download of you two going at it?" She laughed harshly.

"That's enough, Maddie. It's embarrassing enough as it is." Lightchurch was not smiling. "If Robert hadn't boffed her, as you call it, we wouldn't know about the men at the sports facility, would we? And maybe she'll turn into a valuable asset."

Madeline said, "Isn't that what you said the other day? You were going to work your asset?" She laughed out loud and slapped the table with her hand. The two men looked away and said no more.

***

Wilson looked out the window of his hotel room at the black freighter, still at anchor, unmoving. He wished he had more information on its purpose. He could see men moving about on the deck, working by some containers with torches. There were two men working on one of the cranes again.

He turned on the television to watch the news and caught a breaking story about the volcano. It had been erupting violently, spewing so much lava onto the seafloor that it had built up a hundred feet of thickness near the active vent. So much gas was released that it had reached the sea's surface, creating a yellow-brown cloud of toxic fumes above the water. The wind blew the gas cloud toward the northwest shore of the island. As a result, the government had expanded the shipping exclusion zone to fifteen miles and had sent two coastal patrol boats north to patrol the margin of the zone and to warn people to stay away. They were preparing to evacuate those who lived on the nearby coast.

Wilson walked down to the beach bar a half hour before he was to meet Vargas. He had the hotel umbrella with him to ward off the intense rainfall. It had been storming all day, and he could hear the waves crashing onto the beach outside the bar. The side streets had been flowing five inches deep with storm runoff that came down the mountainside as he drove over from the warehouse. Grand Anse Road had been equally flooded. Between the volcano and the storm, it seemed that all hell had broken loose on the island.

Oliver Morant was at the bar checking the liquor inventory and ordering booze for the next few days. He smiled when he saw Wilson and came over to his side of the bar.

"Mr. Wilson, how have you been? I missed you yesterday."

"Good evening, Oliver. I've been busy lately but doin' fine." He shook hands with the bar manager. "I wondered if we have anything we should worry about with so much rain. Will we be flooded here at the hotel?"

"No, no. When they built the hotel, they raised the land where all the buildings are. It may flood all around us, but we will keep our feet dry." He chuckled. "But the power is another matter. We have lost power during storms before." Then his face brightened. "If so, we have a mighty generator."

Gordon overheard this statement. "Yes, but last time the generator stopped working during the night. Scared the hell out of some of our guests."

Morant did not like being corrected. "Yes, but we have a new generator now, don't we, Gordon?"

"Yes, sir. Let's hope we don't need it."

"I hope we don't get too much rain. The streets are already flowing curb deep." Wilson changed the subject.

"Excuse me, Mr. Wilson. I must go call in an order. We runnin' low on gin, vermouth, and Stag." Morant walked briskly out of the bar to his office.

"You hear the latest?" Gordon asked. "Dey had some problem wid the votin' machines today." He leaned in close to whisper to Wilson. "Yeah, they had a problem wid the internet connection."

"What do you mean? They're still voting, aren't they?" Today was the election day for the island's police force. It was the test run before Tuesday's election.

"Yeah, but they got reports that the machines been locking up sometimes. It made the officials go to a manual count," Gordon said.

"But they don't count until the end of the day, do they?"

"Normally, no. But some machines seemed froze up when they fed in the ballots. They tried scanning the ballots again, but the results made no sense. So dey decided on a manual count for now. Maybe fix the problem by Tuesday."

"Wow! That's a problem," Wilson said. He wondered why the machines were having problems, especially since they were new.

"The company that made de machines had a technician there. He say the internet connection was unstable, but that is the way it be here. Always lines down with the rain."

A bright flash of lightning lit up the whole waterfront, followed by a huge crash. One of the palm trees right in front of the hotel burst into flames from being hit by a lightning bolt. Two customers who were sitting at a tall table near the front of the bar jumped and fell to the ground. Gordon and three customers ran over to help them get up from the floor. They were unhurt but scared to death by the sudden bolt so close by. They retreated to the bar and ordered fresh drinks.

Gordon came back with a gin and tonic for Wilson. "There is one other thing that is happenin' dat is strange." He had a conspiratorial look in his eye. "The FM radio station, Radio Free Grenada, is having trouble gettin' signal through. They say the government be jammin' their signal because they pro-GPC an' de government is NSP. Ol' Malcolm say it not so, but nobody believin' him. He say it's de storm."

"Who's Malcolm?" Wilson looked confused.

"Malcolm Churchill is prime minister now. He runnin' against Senjai of the GPC again. People say he going to lose this time, even wid his lies."

Wilson was surprised by this analysis. "He's lying too? Senjai's lying? Churchill said that the government has discovered oil just off the coast somewhere. That should be good news for Grenada, isn't it?"

"Dat what I mean." Gordon's eyes widened. He put his hands in the air and looked up at the ceiling. "He say we found oil in every election. He saying it now too? That's a lie." Gordon shook his head, and his voice conveyed his disbelief.

"Does the radio station lose signal often? Maybe it's the storm." Wilson tried finishing that part of the conversation.

"Mr. Wilson, we have storms here all de time and never a problem like this. Some people say maybe it de new airport radar or something else jammin' up the airwaves, but it ain't because of no storm."

"I heard on the radio that they're testing the new equipment at the airport. Maybe that's the problem." Wilson checked his watch. Vargas was running late. They had planned on an early dinner and then entertainment afterward, but it looked like they weren't going anywhere with the heavy rain. They might have to stay at the hotel and listen to the calypso band playing in the main bar. It was a good band, but he had heard it several times now. That assumed the band could get to the hotel during this storm.

There was a commotion in the hallway just off the bar where one walkway joined the open area next to the pool. Someone had arrived, and he was not in a good mood. "Fucking umbrella." A few people in the bar chuckled at the comment, having wrestled with one of the frustrating things at one time or another.

Tim Martin entered the bar, tossed a half-open umbrella on the floor next to the umbrella rack, and sputtered about how fucking wet it was outside. He stepped into the room, looked around, and spotted Wilson sitting at the bar. He sloshed over on soggy feet that actually made squeegee-like sounds as he walked.

"Hi, Robert," he said, waving his arms in front of him. "I waded over here from the mall in that damn rain. I almost fell into a ditch on the way!" he shouted, outraged. "And a car almost ran over me on the main road out here." He took off his soaked raincoat and threw it over one of the barstools.

"Geez, Tim," Wilson said as Martin squeezed water out of his shirtsleeve. "How'd you get so wet? Why not take a taxi?"

"Couldn't find one. They all shut down, I think." He turned to the barman. "Hey, can I get a shot of bourbon? Make it a double." He plopped down on the stool next to Wilson.

"And where have you been on this fine day?" Wilson asked, grinning and expecting a colorful download of misery.

"Me?" Martin welcomed the opening to speak. "I've been downtown at GPC headquarters all afternoon, working sources." He turned toward Wilson and rolled his eyes. "Man, all hell is going on down there. They got people running around all over the island doing shit." The bourbon arrived and he took a quaff. "And then I waited at the bus stop like a dolt for a good half hour in this damn downpour before getting a number one bus back here to the mall. It took an hour driving here because of all the stalled cars on the road."

"But they could have dropped you out front of the hotel."

"They had to drive around the back way because the driver was afraid we'd get stuck in that big dip coming off the roundabout. Water two feet deep, he said." He slammed down the rest of his drink and ordered another. He leaned in to whisper to Wilson. "Hey, see those two Chinese guys who just came into the bar?" He nodded toward two men in very wet raincoats who entered the bar and seemed to be lurking. "I'm not sure, but I think they've been following me. I saw them twice today."

Wilson looked over at the men, who immediately turned toward the pool; one pointed to the broken palm tree on the beach. "Yeah, I see them."

"I gotta talk to you about something. Maybe tomorrow." He leaned in and whispered. "I finally got ahold of some financial records, and, quite frankly, I can't make hide nor hair of them." He looked cautiously at his fellow journalist. "Remember I said I could get the dope on financing?" He gave Wilson a meaningful stare and a slight grin to sell it. "Well, I got it."

Wilson twisted around on his stool and stared at Martin. "You got it. What do you mean?"

"I have this woman contact in the GPC HQ who is quite friendly, and she made me a copy."

"How many pages is it? How do you know it's the right stuff?"

"Oh, let me tell you. It's the right stuff. Even I can tell that." He smirked confidently. "But I need help with the details. Account numbers, transfer codes, all that shit." He looked angry. "I can't figure it out. But you know that stuff, right?"

"Yeah, I do. At least most of it." Wilson was surprised and impressed. "When can I look at it?"

"Well, you promised you'd look it over for me, remember? I need your help right away to get the scoop." Martin smiled as the next bourbon arrived. "I'll even cut you in on the byline if you help me write it up tomorrow."

Wilson listened carefully, then stopped with his glass halfway to his mouth. "Wait a minute, Tim. If what you say is true—and I believe you—then you're sitting on dynamite." He started thinking through what had to be done. This information could be scandalous.

"Yeah, I know."

Now Wilson leaned into Martin to whisper. "No, you don't. If you have what I think you have, you need to be very careful. It could be dangerous. Nobody wants that kind of info out on the street and certainly not in the newspaper." He pulled away and stared at Martin to see if he understood.

Martin gulped down a slug of whiskey. "What do you mean?"

"Where's the document?"

"Right here." He tapped his shirt pocket, a smirk on his face. "It's on a thumb drive."

Wilson could see that Martin had no idea what could happen. "Here's what you do, Tim. Make a printout of everything, make a backup of the thumb drive, and then have the hotel manager lock up the drive in the safe. Put it inside something so that he can't tell what it is, OK?" He thought about it a moment. "Hell, make two printouts. Mail one to your office right away. We'll need the other copy for work tomorrow. I'm busy tonight or I'd come with you and start work on it now. But I can't change my plans."

"OK. That sounds good." Martin eyed Wilson suspiciously. "You really think it could be dangerous?"

"Absolutely," Wilson warned. "And don't tell anyone what you have. Especially those guys." He glanced toward the two Chinese businessmen. He wondered who they were. He had seen one of them in the bar before. But now they did seem to be watching Martin. *What did Tim get himself into here?* he thought.

Tori Vargas stepped into the bar wearing a small and sexy black cocktail dress. It revealed all her best features, including the radiant smile on her face. Wilson stood up. She came over and gave him a short but sensual kiss on the lips that took his breath away.

"Hello, Roberto. It is so good to see you." She slid onto the stool next to him and frowned. "Who is your soggy friend here?" She smiled at Martin.

"Oh, Ms. Vargas, this is Tim Martin. Another journalist. You're going to be hearing a lot about him soon. Just watch."

She shook Martin's damp hand and then turned back to Wilson.

"Maybe we could sit on one of those lounge chairs for a while. It would be more comfortable for me." She stood up next to him and pointed with her clutch toward the low loungers that were usually only placed by the pool but had been moved in out of the rain.

"OK, sure," he said.

Martin stood up and threw down the last of his bourbon. "Well, I'd better get out of these wet clothes and do what you suggested." He leaned into Wilson. "You lucky dog." He shuffled away toward the business services area of the hotel.

"What will you have to drink? A rum punch?" He grinned at her in a conspiratorial manner. "I know you like them."

She slapped his arm and giggled. "Roberto, you are being a devil." She led them to the loungers, and Wilson passed her order on to the barman. They settled into the chairs, one on each side of a small glass table, waiting for her drink to arrive. She stretched her long legs out on the chaise, displaying her bronze thighs, knowing how distracting it would be for Wilson.

The storm intensified, winds howling through the trees and peppering them with occasional sprays of rainy mist. The warm moisture felt good against his skin.

"I planned to take you out to the Cinnamon Tree Inn for dinner, but the weather is ferocious. We may get stuck on the flooded streets. What do you want to do?" Wilson asked. "Go out or eat inside in the main dining room here?"

"I feel adventurous tonight, Roberto. I would like the Cinnamon Tree if you are not afraid to drive in this hurricane." She laughed lightly. "It is supposed to be very nice there. Very romantic." She leaned toward him and batted her eyelashes.

"Let's be romantic tonight, then." He raised his glass to her and they sipped their drinks. The wind came up and the rain blew directly onto them, so they moved off the loungers and to a couch by the bar for a short time. At 7:00 p.m., they walked through the inner courtyard of the hotel, and Wilson had a valet get his car from the parking area. Within minutes they were sloshing up Morne Rouge Road toward the Cinnamon Tree. The rain let up for a few minutes as they climbed the hill, and they could see the rough sea in the lightning strikes as they drove. The sea was covered with whitecaps at the crest of the huge waves.

Chapter 12

Sunday

They were seated in the main dining room at the inn, where a quartet was playing classic smooth jazz. They sat in a cozy booth built for lovers to be close together, nearly touching. The booth faced the quartet, and they ordered a bottle of Chilean red wine, a merlot, before dinner.

"Roberto, this is very nice and romantic, is it not?" She purred her satisfaction. She leaned against him and they kissed warmly. "I am glad we came here instead of eating at that dreary hotel." She touched his knee under the table.

"I agree. I have eaten there so many times, I'm also glad for a change. And with such a beautiful woman." He grinned at her and she blushed.

She leaned in and kissed him again. "I have a surprise for you." She reached her hand down between his legs, and he intercepted her prowling fingers, surprised at her familiarity. "Take it from me and hide it, but don't let anyone see." She pulled his head to her and kissed him deeply as a distraction as she passed him something small and hard.

He kissed her warmly as he fingered the item and realized it was a thumb drive. He carefully pushed the drive into his pants pocket without looking at it and without releasing her lips. *It's a great kiss anyway,* he thought. *Why stop now?*

She released his neck, and he straightened up in his seat. "That was quite a kiss." He said it out loud, aware that several people were watching them. A young couple at a nearby table giggled and clapped their hands softly. He smiled at them sheepishly and looked at his date.

"What is it?" he whispered.

"I will tell you later. Protect it with your life. They would kill me if they knew what I just did." She cringed as she tried to smile. "I hope it will all be OK for us."

For us, he thought. *She's getting serious or I'm getting seriously played.* He wondered what was happening, a little confused by her sudden gift. He opened his menu to cover his surprise. "They have many good dishes here." He perused the menu. "They have curried shrimp over rice with callaloo sauce. I've had callaloo before; it's really tasty."

"Oh, that sounds wonderful, but I think I may have the crab cake appetizer first and then the mahi-mahi appetizer." She looked at Wilson for his approval. "Is that too much?"

"No, no. Not at all. Order whatever you would like." He knew she could not finish all that food, but he would help her with some of the fish if need be.

They ordered their meals and listened to the quartet, snuggling against each other until their dinners arrived. Wilson was enjoying this close relationship more than he expected. He didn't have to pretend he liked the woman. She was quite endearing on her own. He wasn't sure where this would lead, but he would enjoy her company while it lasted.

"They are here, watching," she said pleasantly as she stared into his eyes.

"What do you mean?" He began to swivel his head. "Where?"

"Don't look right at him." Her face was deadly serious now. "See the tall man with a mustache by the bar?"

Wilson turned his head as if looking for the server. It was the same man he had seen at the sports facility. "Oh, him. Isn't that Cortez?"

"Yes, and there is another man out by the pool too. You can't see him now, but I recognize him."

"Why are they following you?"

"They always watch me. But we left the hotel, so they sent two men to be sure not to lose us."

"Shit. I don't like being watched."

"Me neither. But it is part of my life." Her eyes teared up, sadness just beneath the surface of her lovely face.

"Why Cortez? Isn't he too important to spend time on surveillance?"

"He has a special interest in you and me. He thinks we're enjoying the sex too much. He told me this during our meeting today."

"Why should he care? You're just another agent to him, aren't you?"

"He likes me in his own wicked way. He hurt me today because he thinks I like you too much. But I told him it was all an act to get you involved with me. To make you love me." Her eyes turned to Wilson's, asking his understanding. "I do like you, Roberto. I might even be . . . Well, love is another thing, is it not?" Her eyes were a mystery. Pain? Love? Fear?

"And we just kissed in public," Wilson said, now worried. "Won't look good to him then." Wilson wondered what to do. The woman was growing on him. He didn't want her hurt. What would Cortez do?

Wilson's phone beeped an incoming call. He looked at the screen and recognized Pendergast's number. *What timing.*

"Hey, I need to take this, Tori. My editor." He raised his eyebrows. "OK?"

"Yes, talk to the man. I will wait right here." She smiled weakly and lifted her wine glass, looking miserable and joyful at the same time.

He got up from the table and walked over to the edge of the patio near the pool. He saw a furtive man in the shadows there, possibly the other man spying on Vargas, so he moved to the entryway for privacy, still keeping Vargas in sight. "Hello, Jimmy. What do you have for me?"

"We need to talk in person. I have new info on our friends and can't talk about it on the phone." He paused. "Where are you right now? Can we meet?"

"I'm in the middle of something. Can't get away now. Can it wait till tomorrow?"

"Guess it'll have to. How about an early meet?"

"That would work. Where and when?"

"Eight a.m., my place."

"Sounds good." He hung up the call and looked over at Vargas, who was staring at him. She smiled. He smiled back. Then he noticed Cortez staring across the restaurant at her too. He was grim-faced, and his angry, dark eyes were focused tightly. *Not good,* he thought. Wilson looked around the pool for the other guy and caught only a view of his silhouette as he retreated down the steps to the driveway.

Wilson walked back to the table. Their food had arrived, and they had a wonderful meal. By the time they finished, it was 10:00 p.m. and the music was wrapping up for the night. They walked out to the entry, and he gave the valet his stub for the car.

***

The rain was subdued on their drive back to the hotel. The streets were still flooded, and they crept along on their adventure through black water. They saw one car along the way that had overshot the turn in front of the hotel and was now half floating in the roadside drainage ditch. Wilson had seen a snake in the ditch on previous occasions. They passed it and drove into the car park after Leslie let them through the gate. They disembarked, and he carried his briefcase with them into the hotel.

"I have a surprise for you, Tori. Why don't you come up to my room and stay the night?"

She looked up at him, and her eyes showed delight at the suggestion. "Oh, Roberto. That would be nice. But we must talk a little before we get there. They probably have your room bugged too."

"OK, let's talk here first." He led her to one of the small sitting areas in the middle of the hotel garden. It was a small gazebo-like structure with soft seats inside. He made sure that no one was within earshot, but then decided they would be better off in the bar, with the sea and raucous chatter of other customers providing a background din.

"OK," she said. "Then you can buy me another of those lovely rum punches since you will have your pleasure with me anyway." She giggled. "I look forward to it, Roberto." She suddenly turned serious and came close to nibble his ear and whisper into it. "I have given you copies of all the personnel files I have access to here in Grenada. It has their service records and ranks—everything about them."

Wilson was not sure he heard her correctly. He pulled back to let it sink in. Then he leaned in again.

"What? Really? That's great, Tori," he whispered back. "But why now? You could have waited to see how well we treat you before you gave away so much."

"It is because I trust you, Roberto. I think I . . .Well, you know how I feel."

"For what it's worth, I brought you evidence that I am indeed a writer, a journalist, and a historian. Here is the material to show Cortez as proof." He reached inside his briefcase for the manila envelope and handed it to her. "I don't want anything to happen to you." He meant that.

"Oh, that is nice. I think maybe tomorrow I can get more files from one of the other computers. There may be more about Cortez and his mission."

"No. Not now, Tori. If you got caught, they would know we have this info, too, and it would make it less useful. Do you understand?" She looked confused and a little hurt that he was refusing her help. "We can do only a little at a time or it will look suspicious."

She listened to him, sad at first, but then she brightened. "One more thing. Whatever is going to happen will be on Tuesday night. That is all I know." Her mischievous smile returned. "Now we can go to your room."

He put an arm around her and kissed her. Then, without changing position, he said, "I have a surprise for you. I have a machine that can cancel out any recording in the room. A friend of mine from the newspaper sent it to me. I just plug it in, and it makes a swarm of radio waves that will jam any signal sent from the room. So they can't hear us or see us tonight once it comes up to power. It takes two minutes to get strong enough to jam their signal. That way it seems like a natural interference. Pretty clever, isn't it."

"Now you tell me you have spy tools." A questioning look. "What do I believe now?"

"No, no." He shook his head and put up his hands. "My journalist friend worked in Russia for a year, and he had this machine with him because everyone knows the Russians spy on everybody there. He didn't want them listening to him talk to his sources or they would arrest them. That's all."

She seemed reassured but did not smile. They sat there a few more moments, each sipping a drink. Finally, she said, "I believe you. Even if you are a spy, I have to trust you."

They walked to the door of his room, and he put the key in the lock. He reached into the briefcase and flipped the switch on a small black box. He pushed the door open and turned on the light. They entered, and he had her stand by the door while he walked quickly into the bathroom, making sure they were alone. They didn't say anything important until two minutes had expired. Then they acted like normal lovers would in a hotel room.

Later, as Tori slept quietly, he left the bed and walked to the balcony door. The rain had picked up again, and thunder boomed across the bay. Large waves crashed on the beach, adding their rumble to the night's torment. Through it all, he could see the mooring lights of the black freighter, lying in wait.

Chapter 13

Monday

The next morning, Wilson left the hotel after spending the night with Tori Vargas in his room. It was a memorable date for many reasons. One of these reasons was pressing on his mind at seven in the morning when she had crept off to her own room to shower and prepare for her day of conference proceedings. This reason was on a small thumb drive. He took the drive with its purloined files with him as he drove around the flooded streets for twenty minutes, making sure he was not being followed. After last night, he felt that Cortez might be on to him.

Something was troubling him. He knew he had to take advantage of his relationship with Vargas for the good of the mission. But that was the problem. He had a relationship with her, not just a role where he acted out his part to get information from her. He found her pleasant to be with, not just the sex but the woman herself. Maybe it was foolish, but he wondered if they might be able to maintain the relationship after the mission was finished. It sounded stupid, but he enjoyed her simple and straightforward charm. And he wanted to help her. The thought occupied the back of his mind as he drove through the wet streets.

At the warehouse, he had enough time to insert the thumb drive into his USB port and verify that there were no viruses on the device. He and Madeline looked the files over for a few minutes and found that the material was as Vargas had said, personnel files and other information about the conference and the people who had come to Grenada from Venezuela. One file in particular caught Wilson's attention; it was that of Major Fernando Cortez, leader of Operation Condor.

"Holy shit!" he said. "This is really bad. Just the name tells us something about the operation. It's major league trouble."

"Bugger. You're right. Either she's handed us a false lead or we're onto something big. I'll call Lightchurch now." She touched a button on her phone keypad, completely absorbed.

It was nearly 8:00 a.m., and he had to meet Pendergast at his shop. He was also going to help Tim Martin with his financial data later in the day. He had Madeline take over the examination of the files and asked her to keep him informed. She also said with a smirk that she would wait until later and ask how his date went. Her eyes registered disapproval, maybe something more. He left the warehouse in a huff.

Wilson decided to drive along the flooded Grand Anse Road, stopping at the Spiceland Mall shopping center, where he parked the car and proceeded on foot through the stores, avoiding any tails. He took the opportunity to call Martin and to tell him he would meet him later because something had come up. He told him to get started reviewing the data in his room and not to leave the hotel under any circumstances until Wilson returned.

He wandered through a few shops, stopping for coffee and a sweet roll at one of the coffee shops in the mall, before working his way out the back and to the car again. He hustled but still arrived at the Reefer shop twenty minutes late.

He saw Pendergast out on his dock next to his thirty-foot Sportcraft. He rushed down the dock and heard a gruff, "You're late!"

Pendergast turned around and gave him a scowl that stopped him in his tracks. "Damn it, man. We gotta shove off right now. I'll tell you on the way."

Wilson jumped over the gunwale right behind Pendergast while Wet Dog started the engines. Within seconds they had backed off the dock, and Wet Dog turned the boat out to sea. They came up to speed fast and veered left toward Quarantine Point. The sea was still choppy after the storm, with large swells that lifted them as they motored along. The sky had cleared temporarily, but huge roll clouds still filled the horizon as the storm drifted to the south.

"The damn Russians left during the night," Pendergast shouted over the noise of the wind and the slapping waves. "I had a man there after dark, but he left the lookout on Quarantine Point at midnight. This morning they were gone. Must have set sail in the night when the storm slackened. They may have as much as an eight-hour head start on us."

"But where would they go?" Wilson asked. "Why leave so abruptly?"

"We don't know, but they were up to something. Of that I'm certain."

They rounded the point; the wave height increased, so they reduced speed. Wet Dog swore like a sailor and fought the waves. Rain began falling again, limiting their visibility dramatically. The wind changed direction and became gusty. The boat began taking water over the starboard bow. Wet Dog cut back and changed his course to ride the waves differently, without sloshing the sea onto their decks.

Pendergast pulled on a life jacket, and so did Wet Dog. Wilson looked around for another but found none. Wet Dog shouted to him. "You can swim, can't ya?"

Both Pendergast and Wet Dog laughed like it was the funniest thing they had ever heard. "Your face tells a real tale, Robert." They laughed until a wave crashed over the bow and they were all soaked with seawater. Wet Dog handed Wilson a life jacket.

"We'll run west for a ways and then cut south to Canoe Bay and around the point," Pendergast said. "They were out there the last few days. Maybe they moved the ship there to cut the travel time back and forth."

Wet Dog brought them in closer to the coast near Canoe Bay. They could see the shoreline then, and he reduced speed for a while as they neared Point Salines. The wind rose to near gale force, and huge waves crashed on the rock of the promontory. They could see a large flashing red light on the end of the point where a self-sustained lighthouse marked the treacherous waters. Next to the lighthouse was a huge radar station with a revolving dish that searched the skies for any threat of aircraft.

"That's the new radar the Russians set up last year. They installed four new stations: one here, one at Grand Etang in the middle of the island, one north of Saint George's, and one across the island. It improved radar control for the airport." Pendergast seemed pleased. "We needed an upgrade on that system. The Cubans built the original with Soviet parts, so it failed often." He laughed. "But it lasted quite a few years even then."

"It was a hell of an engineering project to site them stations," Wet Dog said. "The Russians had the whole point dug up anchoring the damn thing. Even running cables out into the sea as anchors. This one station took almost as long as the other three stations combined."

"And they lost two men out here during construction. Both drowned while doing underwater construction. It was a terrible thing," Pendergast said solemnly.

"OK, we're comin' round the point, and the seas are goin' to be a little rough," Pendergast shouted. A wave slapped over the gunnel and soaked Wilson in one go. He gripped the railing on the cabin and moved inside. Pendergast shouted some orders to Wet Dog and then came under the canopy too.

"Jimmy," Wet Dog called out. "We're almost on the last point of contact. I'll reduce speed and try radar."

Pendergast looked doubtful. "The damn thing probably won't work for this. Too weak of a signal." He made a fist. "The fuckers got away. They must have suspected somethin'."

"Made contact—a half mile out. Coming on a new course."

"I spoke too soon," Pendergast shouted. "Slow, slow, Wet Dog. And watch your visibility." He looked at Wilson. "We don't want him seeing us nosing around. We aren't rigged for a fight."

"A fight? Why a fight?" Wilson asked, caught off guard at the sudden possibility.

"If you were up to no good and a nosey boat came on you doing it, would you let them get home to talk about it?"

"Oh shit!"

"Exactly," Pendergast said, pulling out a Colt .45 semiautomatic pistol from a pouch on the console. He pulled the slide back a quarter inch to check that he had a round in the barrel. He noticed Wilson watching him. "I'd rather be prepared in case we see trouble."

"Won't they see us if we can see them?"

"We're pretty small on any radar screen. So we should be OK as long as we don't go runnin' into them." He looked a Wet Dog and shouted to get his attention. "Right, Wet Dog?"

"Yes, sir." He cut the speed again, grinning madly.

"Cut the engine. Eyes to starboard." Pendergast used a pair of binoculars for several minutes, scanning the mist for the starboard side of the boat. Wilson wondered if he could see anything in the dense haze.

They drifted in the waves and listened. In the distance, they heard the rattle of an outboard motor and a man shouting. Then, on their right side, they glimpsed a tall ship through a break in the rain. It was there for only a second, but they all saw it.

Pendergast whispered, "There they are. Wet Dog, get a GPS read on this location." He turned to Wilson. "We'll keep an eye on them until the storm sets in again." Then to Wet Dog he said, "Don't let us drift in on them. Use the electric motor for positioning."

They drifted there, occasionally seeing the tall masts or the hull of *Varoushka* but never the whole ship in one view. At one point, a small boat came toward them, and they held their breaths for a few seconds.

Then the rain came in hard again and the wind picked up. Pendergast sniffed the air and felt the sea under them. "Boys, we're getting out of here. It's goin' to get rough real quick."

Wet Dog started the engines and brought them about, headed back toward the point. Pendergast directed him. "Head for the point. If it gets too rough, we'll go along the south shore to True Blue Bay if we can make it."

They motored along in silence as Wet Dog did his magic and fought the sea. Their speed was better than before because they ran partway with the waves. Finally, they made the point, and Pendergast decided they would risk returning the way they had come. They had to fight the sea, running up oncoming waves and then crashing down the backside, jarring them on each drop. Their true speed was poor, as they gained only a few feet with each wave. After what seemed like an hour of this shuddering struggle, they had to head diagonally up the waves as they changed course.

The boat made a vicious and sickening roll with each wave. You had to really like the ocean to deal with this chaos.

It took nearly three hours to get back to the dock and tie up the boat. They encountered no other boats at all on their course.

They were all soaked, and even though the weather was not cold, they were chilled and dehydrated. Pendergast passed out Stag beers, and they huddled around the small space heater to dry out their clothes. He turned on the local radio station, letting it blare over the wind. One of the GPC political ads ran between every song or announcement.

"What were they doing?" asked Wilson. "And why in the storm?"

"I don't know. I have to check the marine charts and see what's out that far west on Shark Reef. There's some deep water farther out."

Wet Dog murmured, "Maybe there's a ship down there we don't know about."

The radio announcer broke with a news alert. The storm had now been classified as Tropical Storm Betty. She might grow into a category one hurricane if winds continued strengthening.

Wilson jumped up. "Damn! It's after two. I have to go." He said his goodbyes and raced outside to the Noah, a perfect name for a vehicle in this weather. He climbed in and turned the key. Nothing. The battery was completely dead. *That's all I need—a dead battery.* Anger overcame him. He walked back through the water to the Reefer shop, swearing out loud.

"Can you drive me to Spiceland? My car's out of commission. The battery is as dead as a doornail." He swore some more. "I have to get back to the hotel and meet someone."

"I can't spare a man now," Pendergast said as he stood up and fished for a set of keys in his desk drawer. "From the looks of these waves, we need to move our boats into the lagoon to protect them from the storm. You can take my extra truck and leave your rental here. The truck has better clearance anyway. You'll need it the way the water's rising."

Chapter 14

Monday

Wilson arrived at the car park at 2:30 p.m., fighting through torrential rain the whole way. Pendergast was right; the car could never have made it through the flooded streets, which were now deeper than before. As it was, cars were abandoned along the side of the road, and many people were stranded while trying to get home. He hoped the rental didn't float away during the storm. A few of the small local buses still bravely plowed through the water, but soon only boats would travel the streets.

Leslie greeted him at the hotel gate. "Good afternoon, Mr. Wilson. We got a righteous storm on us today." The man wore white rubber Wellington boots and was standing in about seven inches of water.

"No kidding, Leslie. Is the whole property flooded?"

"No, sir," he said. "The main building area is still dry for now. The storm surge is climbin' up the beach, and they closing down the beach bar now. They also closing up the seawall as they prepare for Betty."

"I was meeting someone in the bar."

"They all moved to the main bar now. Go see Gordon there. He's lookin' for you."

"OK. Thanks, Leslie. When do you go home?"

"I can't get home now, so I stay and help the hotel and our guests. You stay safe now, Mr. Wilson." He waved the truck through to the car park as a delivery van pulled up to the gate.

Wilson decided he would stop at the mall and get a pair of Wellingtons for himself as soon as he could. But the mall would probably close for the storm. Now that Tropical Storm Betty had been announced, there would be a run on food and supplies, although not like in the States where everyone panicked at the mention of bad weather.

He slogged through the water to the main building complex and his room. The rain was still coming down steadily, in sheets like it had at sea. In his room, he stripped off his wet clothing and shoes. He dropped them on the floor and looked out the window. There lay the black freighter, taunting him in its way, still at anchor and still an enigma. She had her mooring lights on even in the daytime. She shifted uneasily in the storm.

He checked the room to be sure everything was the same as when he had left with Vargas in the morning. Nothing looked out of place. Then he remembered he had left his jamming device running in the briefcase all day. He checked whether it was still operating but found that the battery had died. He would need new batteries if he planned to bring Vargas up to bed again tonight.

He wondered how her day was going. He hoped they would be able to get together and talk about what lay ahead for her as an agent. And as a friend and lover. Then he caught himself. *None of that, Robert. You have to let that go. Be professional.*

He took a quick, hot shower and then dressed in dry clothes. He pulled on an extra shirt. He noted that even in the tropics, it can seem cold once you get used to the daily heat. He left the room and walked to the main bar, where he looked for Gordon. Luckily, Gordon was bartending, so he took a stool and waved to him.

"How are you, Mr. Wilson? I heard you went out early today." He grinned. "No stay in wid your lady friend?" He winked at Wilson.

"No. That would have been nice, but I had a meeting." He tried deflecting the subject. "But now that you mention her, have you seen Ms. Vargas today?"

"Not since lunch. We served lunch at the conference room, but there was hardly anyone there. I guess the storm kept dem away," he said. "They may cancel the rest of the meetings because of Betty."

"Makes sense to me. If you see her, let her know I asked. OK?"

"I got news on that radio trouble for you." He leaned across the bar, a sign he had some juicy rumor. "Radio Free Grenada is off the air. No one knows why. One man say the cable supportin' the antenna was cut during the storm and the whole thing fall into the jungle up there at Grand Etang. Nobody saying otherwise, unless they be more jammin' and such."

"You're kidding. That sounds just crazy." Wilson wasn't sure why the station had gone off the air, but it was more likely that the storm had damaged the antenna than sabotage.

"No. You don't believe me, but it true. RFG is the only independent radio station on this island. In the whole country. All other stations are government stations. They control all airwaves here. If you want to control the island, you must control the media. So you take out the only independent radio." He shook his head. To him it was obvious that the government had shut down the station.

Wilson suddenly sat upright. Of course, if you were planning a coup, you would need control over the media first. That was how coups were done.

"Hey, let me use the house phone, will you?" He had to talk to Martin. Gordon brought over a phone, and Wilson had the resort operator call Martin's room. He got him on the line.

"Where you been, Wilson?" Martin was in a pissy mood. "I've been working my ass off up here and you didn't show up and help. What gives?"

"I got stuck on a mission this morning. I'm here now and ready to work all night if necessary. OK?" He felt the tension ease up a bit on Martin's end of the conversation. "Have you eaten lunch? I was going to grab a sandwich in the bar."

"No, and I'm famished." His voice brightened at the prospect of a sandwich and a drink. "I'll be right down. Main bar, right? They closed the beach bar."

Martin arrived, and they took a table at the back so that they could talk. They ordered lunch and coffee, then caught up on the financials.

"We definitely have something big here," Martin whispered, looking around to make sure that no one was listening. "I got hundreds of contributions right at the campaign limit, all deposited in batches to three bank accounts. I can't get past those accounts, but the numbers are really fishy." Martin fussed over his morning's work.

"What do you mean by fishy?"

"The ledger shows some twelve thousand donations from individuals on the island. All those donations are for the maximum individual amount allowed, one thousand Eastern Caribbean dollars, about four hundred fifty US dollars. But if you look at the income of the entire population of Grenada, a total of about one hundred and seven thousand people, there aren't that many people on the island who could make that kind of donation." He raised his eyebrows and stared at Wilson for effect. "And then there are donations from people outside the country. There are many citizens living in Miami, Toronto, and Britain. They can all still vote and contribute, right?"

"OK," Wilson agreed. "So they send money home to the party of their choice too."

Their food arrived and they dove into it. They were both ravenous.

"Right," Martin said. "But the records show more contributions coming in from overseas than there are citizens overseas. And all those donations are at the limit too . . . I mean, they can't all be voting for the GPC and none voting for the NSP, can they?"

"You're really on to something." Wilson whistled softly. "But where is the money coming from?"

"Three accounts so far, but I can't tell where from."

"Let's finish up here and get started on the data," Wilson said. "Let me make a call, then I'm free." He stepped away from the table and dialed Madeline. She answered on the third ring. "Hey, it's me. I have a lot of news to share with you," he said.

"Me too. But not on an open line," she said. "Where are you?"

"I'm at the hotel meeting with Martin about some financial info he has. I'm going to be tied up all afternoon and probably into the night." He hesitated. "Can you come out here and talk? The water in the street is pretty deep, though."

"I can make it, but I'll need an hour or so. I'll call you when I get there."

"Good."

Martin and Wilson finished their meals and walked to Martin's room with their coffee cups, ready for a long afternoon. When they arrived, Wilson saw sheets of paper with dense rows of numbers covering the bed, the dresser, and all the other surfaces. Martin had them organized by month and account, but he had only just started on tracking the payments. They set about doing just that.

Wilson began by identifying the bank routing codes and transfer numbers that occurred most frequently in the listings.

He realized that in order to do that efficiently, he needed his laptop from the warehouse. He called Madeline and asked her to bring it with her to the hotel. Until she arrived, he used pen and paper to write down lists of numbers for correlation.

Madeline arrived after 4:00 p.m. and dropped off the computer. Then she stepped aside with Wilson and discussed what she had found on the thumb drive they had obtained from Tori Vargas. They stood outside Martin's room in the corridor, just out of the rain, and talked when no one came by.

"That woman gave you some great shit," Madeline said appreciatively. "We have the personnel files on every person who is attending the conference and more. It's a great insight into the Department of Social Information, their organization, and many of their projects. It also gives us the structure diagram of the file management system, should we want to hack into it at some time, along with some passwords."

"She said it included useful files," he said. "What else? Anything we can use right now?"

"Yes. It has the name and assignments of the teams that are here for the conference. They're not just here attending meetings." She raised an eyebrow for effect. "They have a plan for reorganizing the government here as directed by someone referred to only as MHS."

"MHS? Minister Hjarad Senjai?"

"Your guess is as good as mine. But I think that makes the most logical sense."

"So they stage a government takeover according to some plan." He stopped and thought about it. What did that mean? How would they take over the government?

"The problem is her files cover only seventy-three individuals, and there were more people than that at the sports facility the other night. I think these are just the ones who received a cover story related to the conference—the ones in the other hotel and here. But some of them used falsified names and passports to enter the country."

"Was she or Cortez mentioned in those files?" he asked, curious.

"She was. She is what she said she is—a glorified secretary and pleasure provider for important members of the Maduro government." Madeline showed a new level of understanding for Vargas and her role. "Imagine the conversations she must have overheard."

"She doesn't like her job. She said she's been forced into it or her family will suffer."

"This seems to confirm much of what she told you. I'm sorry, Robert. I thought she was just a whore."

"She's not like that," he said stiffly.

"Robert, be careful. It's just a job." She put her hand on his arm. "Just be careful. OK? Don't get too involved with her."

Wilson changed the subject back to the men who were not covered by the files. "What does the file say about Cortez?"

"He's a Cuban national who has taken on an important role in the Venezuelan intelligence service. We already know that many of the people in controlling positions in the Maduro government are really Cubans. Cortez is one of the top dogs there."

"What does Lightchurch think about this stuff?"

"He's already planned to bring it up with the Grenada PM at a meeting today. He thinks there's enough here for immediate action. He wants to let the PM know there may be a coup."

"That will go over well on the eve of the national election." Wilson spoke softly, his face slack as he thought.

"What have you learned today from this paper chase?" Madeline stepped closer.

Wilson told her what they had found so far and indicated where they needed help. Madeline said she had a contact in the banking industry who could find out about bank account numbers in the country. He said he would contact Langley about the offshore accounts and transfers. The agency worked with the Treasury Department to track laundered money overseas. They could probably find the source in short order.

Madeline left the resort, and Wilson sent off a request to his control about the account numbers. Then he set about making a simple spreadsheet of the major transactions they could follow. In all, millions of foreign dollars had been funneled into the GPC campaign. But the question remained: Who had made the donations and why?

They worked until 8:00 p.m., manipulating the numbers as much as they could without knowing who owned the bank accounts and who had donated the money. They went to dinner in the dining room and watched the rainfall sweep in off the ocean in dense sheets. Wilson called Vargas's room several times but received no answer. He asked for her at the front desk, but no one had seen her since the conference lunch.

There was little to do after that besides continue working on the financial transactions. They decided to begin writing an article for the *Miami Observer* based on what they knew so far. They would fill in the blanks later and make any changes necessary. At least they would be closer to finishing with a draft article in hand.

Madeline called in at 10:00 p.m. and said that she and Nash had located the Best Beach Hotel where the other Venezuelans were staying and verified that there were fifty-five there and fifteen at the Hempstead, including Vargas. Only some of the people were in their rooms at that time of night, but it was still early.

She also said that Lightchurch had set up a meeting with Prime Minister Malcolm Churchill for later that evening. The PM was preoccupied on the campaign trail, as it was the last night before the election, and had no spare time until then. Lightchurch would inform him of the Venezuelans and the fact that they were there under false pretenses—not for a conference but for a coup d'état. Madeline would be at the meeting to present the information they had already gathered.

Wilson took a break from writing and walked to Vargas's room. He knocked on the door but got no reply. He wondered if she was working late, especially because the rest of the conference may have been canceled. He dashed over to the conference center but found no one there. He saw some literature about the conference on a table by the entryway but no people. There was no notice that tomorrow's meetings were canceled, so he decided he would check with the front desk about what was planned for the next day.

The man at the desk was new to Wilson. He said he had no new information about the conference, but he had been told the decision about whether to cancel would be made the next day. He did not know anything beyond that.

Wilson went back to Martin's room, where they continued to slave away on the article. Just before midnight, Madeline called in again.

"The meeting with the PM went well enough. He was too preoccupied to focus on the news. All he could talk about was a new poll that showed that he and Senjai were nearly tied. He was beside himself." She went on. "When Lightchurch brought up the Venezuelans, he said he thought there must be some mistake. The Venezuelan government had been very supportive of his administration. But he was concerned that so many men had come into the country and were here under assumed names. He said he would discuss it with the minister of justice in the morning."

"Did Lightchurch bring up the arms we found on the Wong site?"

"No." She paused. "He decided the PM was too preoccupied to deal with something that dramatic. He didn't seem to believe anything could be happening."

"But that's an even more important issue," Wilson said.

"He waited to pull the chief of police aside and then told him that he had seen a report that there were shipments of arms appearing on the island," she said. "The man immediately wanted to know who the source of what he called a 'rumor' was. That set Lightchurch back at the start. Then he was concerned that the police may have been compromised. So he dropped the topic."

"Interesting." Wilson contemplated these facts. Could the Venezuelans have part of the police force involved in a coup? That would make it hard to resist a takeover.

Madeline realized he was deep in thought. She asked, "What are you thinking, Robert?" When he didn't reply quickly, she said, "Say, I have that information about local banks for you. Should I text it over?"

"Yeah, please do. We're writing up a storm over here, and it makes a good story. But we must know who is who in order to make sense of it all." Wilson rubbed his eyes. "I can't keep this up too much longer. I need some sleep."

"I'll send it shortly." She ended the call.

He worked for another thirty minutes and then his phone rattled that he had a text. He looked at the numbers and names and told Martin to read over his shoulder. He started writing the information down.

"So the money came from three different accounts, as we thought," he said. "One is from an account controlled by the GPC to its main contributions account."

"OK, let's see." Martin looked at some papers and marked several transactions with a yellow marker. "OK. That checks out."

"Here is another account we've seen a lot," Wilson said. "It's from Commerce Bank and is for many donations. I remember this routing number. Somebody sent money to the campaign, but as we can see here, under a variety of names. But the one account was involved in all the transactions . . . Well, I'll be damned. It's from an account registered to Grenada Construction Company."

"Who are they?"

Wilson moved on, ignoring the question. "And the last number belongs to Melbourne Consulting. I've never heard of them, but they did the same thing as Wong. Lots of contributions that I bet we find come from lots of different names on the ledger books."

"At least we can write that many illegal donations have been made to the GPC party. And I bet we can find that many of the people who donated funds are not real. But we need a lot more research to prove that."

"We won't know more until we get info on the overseas routing numbers," Wilson said, thinking of what they should do next. "Shit. I thought we could wrap this up tonight."

"Me too, but I'm beat. Let's call it a night." Martin began clearing a few papers off his bed. "Maybe a nightcap?"

"Let me send these names off to my editor and see if research comes back with anything. Then I'll join you."

Martin left the room, and Wilson sent an email to Langley. He packed up his computer and decided he should check on

Vargas one more time in case she'd come in late. He walked to her room and knocked on the door. No answer. It was after midnight. She should be in by now.

He stopped at his room and then had second thoughts about leaving his computer there without him, so he entered and checked his room phone for messages. Nothing.

He looked out the window at the passing storm. It was at its peak right now, according to the weather app on his phone. Through the rain, he could still make out the mooring lights of the black freighter at anchor.

He walked down to the main bar and sat next to Martin, who was slurping down a rum punch. Wilson ordered a Glenlivet scotch, neat, and sipped it while Martin told him how much work remained before they could finish the story. Wilson listened half-heartedly; he wasn't interested so much in the story as the underlying source of the money.

After a second drink, Wilson called it a night. He carried his computer back to his room, wondering if he should drive it back to the warehouse so that it would be secure for the night. He was too tired to drive there. He stopped by the front desk again and used the house phone to call Vargas's room. Again, there was no answer.

He walked over and spoke with the night clerk, someone he knew from a daytime shift. "Good night. I just called Ms. Vargas's room and there was no answer."

"Oh, Mr. Wilson, how are you? She was a friend of yours, was she not?"

"Yes. I've been trying to reach her all afternoon but with no luck."

"I assumed you knew. She and several others from the Venezuela conference checked out this afternoon." He paused and smiled at Wilson. "Because of the storm, I think. But I don't know where they would go in this weather."

"Checked out? When?"

"Let's see." He consulted a list. "Just after noon. I remember because she had someone pack up her things for her. She must have been too busy with the conference."

"You mean she's gone?" Wilson practically shouted at the man.

"I'm sorry, Mr. Wilson. She didn't tell you?" The desk clerk was startled at his outburst.

Shocked, Wilson turned away from the desk, mumbling, "Thank you."

He headed for the bar. His head was spinning. *Why hadn't she said something?* There must have been time. Gordon was gone for the night and only one man remained to serve late-night stragglers. He ordered another scotch, Glenlivet, double.

Maybe she was being watched and couldn't get away or leave a message. Maybe they all had to leave on short notice because of the storm. Things were a bit dicey here at the hotel with the storm surge rising. Maybe they had another, safer location to move to.

He had another scotch and then one more as he tried to figure out what could have happened, all while trying to work through his emotions. *He hadn't really cared for her that much, right?* He had known her only a few days. Why did he feel like this? Did she feel the same? Or was it really just an act to draw him in? It certainly worked. He felt defeated and abandoned.

But she had given him information that put her in danger. At least part of it was true. She wanted out of Venezuela. And her parents? He could have Langley check whether they were real, if they did exist in the conditions she claimed. *Then most of her story was true. Right?*

He resolved that he would look for her in the morning. It was too late to go pounding on doors now. *Hell, after 2:00 a.m.* He would catch someone from the Venezuelan delegation in the morning and see where they all went. It would fit her play anyway. She was supposedly bringing him in close, so he would naturally want to find her. Just another lovesick journalist who met a sexy beauty on vacation. *Right?*

The barman said he was going home; the bar was closed. Wilson got up from his stool and signed the bar tab. He stumbled off to his room and collapsed on his bed.

Rain and wind beat a steady drum on his window all night. The black freighter's mooring lights drifted ominously on the dark horizon.

Chapter 15

Tuesday

Election Day began with heavy rain. Wilson listened with closed eyes to a weather report on the television in his room before he got dressed. The worst of the storm had gone north, and there was concern of flooding and heavy storm surge on the sister island of Carriacou, which was lower lying and smaller than Grenada. Rain continued, but the storm surge near Saint George's was receding slightly. In any case, the airport and the harbor were closed. Three days had passed since a cruise ship had docked and that looked like it would continue for at least another few days. Other harbor traffic was limited by the storm.

There were reports of three people who had drowned during the storm. Several others were missing, but the news team hoped for the best. Elections were taking place, with many people braving the elements and turning out to vote in this important event.

The hotel grounds were largely flooded, except the area of the main buildings. Streets all around were swamped. From his hotel window, Wilson could see people walking out by the seawall, looking at the shoreline erosion caused by the storm. Huge waves still crashed on the seawall, sending spray twenty feet into the air. The sun attempted to show itself here and there between the thick black clouds that still drizzled rain on the landscape.

Wilson's head felt like it would explode; the pain behind his eyes was staggering. The light bothered him, reminding him of the scotch he had tossed down last night. His head hurt, and his stomach growled for something that would absorb the alcohol that still polluted his system. He dug in his travel kit for aspirin and swallowed three. He finished dressing and gazed out the window again.

Then he noticed it. The black freighter was gone. He jumped at the sight. After seeing it for so many days in a row, it was like his world was suddenly destabilized and he couldn't get enough air.

Where had it gone?

He grabbed his binos and checked in all directions to see if it had just sailed toward the horizon. But no. It was not in sight.

He packed up his computer, the briefcase, and his handgun before leaving the room. He needed coffee and eggs—no, maybe toast. He would make several calls. He needed to think. He needed his headache to go away. The light hurt his eyes as he stumbled toward the dining room.

He selected a table in the corner of the main dining room, where the buffet was usually served but where only the smaller a la carte menu was being offered today. He ordered black coffee and the continental breakfast, his stomach still a question. After the coffee arrived, he made his first call.

"Jimmy, it's Wilson," he said in an unsteady voice. "The freighter has left its moorings. Do you know anything about it?"

"Morning, Robert. I called earlier. Didn't you get my message?"

Wilson checked his phone. He had missed two messages. "No, I just noticed them now. Did you call about this?"

"No, about the other matter we discussed."

"Oh, that." The Russians. "We need to talk about that later. Unless it's time sensitive?"

"It can keep awhile, I suppose." He paused. "Are you all right? You sound punchy."

"I had a bit of a bout last night. Bad morning."

"Come by and I'll make you my hangover remedy. Fix you right up."

"Maybe." He held his head and sipped coffee. "Hey, can I use your truck today. We're still knee-deep here."

"No problem; no business anyway."

"About the freighter?"

"I'll make some calls and get back to you. Let's meet before noon." He hung up.

Wilson looked at his watch. *Shit!* Almost 10:00 a.m. He had slept too late. He ate several bites of toast with nutmeg jam on it and decided he'd risk a few scrambled eggs. Then he checked his messages again. A call from Madeline. He hit the dial button.

"Robert? Where have you been? I tried to call you earlier."

"I missed it. Running way behind today. What's happening?"

"Shit. You weren't with her again, were you?"

"No, no." He thought of what he should say. "She's gone."

"What? Where'd she go?"

"Just gone."

"You're not making any sense, Robert. Do you mean gone somewhere else? Or gone like dead? Or what? I don't understand." Impatience marred her voice.

"I don't know. She and several others packed up and left yesterday afternoon. I know not where." He realized that in his confusion he was not explaining anything well.

"Robert, you sound funny. Have you been drinking? Oh shit! You broke up with her, didn't you? That's what happened, isn't it?" She sounded both concerned and amused. "Or did she dump you?" Quiet giggling, then silence.

He hadn't thought of that possibility. Maybe that's why he felt so strange. He felt like he had been dumped because it was so sudden. Out of his control.

"Robert? Are you there?" Now she sounded concerned. "What's going on? You can't do this. We need you. Now, damn it!" She shouted these last words, and he pulled the phone farther from his ear.

"I'm OK. I just need some time to get it together. That's all." He wasn't sure he would get it together anytime soon.

"Look, here's what's happening on my end. Overnight the PM decided to act on the information we gave him. He's authorized the police to apply to the chief magistrate for arrest warrants for those Venezuelans we identified yesterday. They're in court right now going through the process. They think they'll have them by noon; then they can act."

"So the police will handle it?"

"Yes. We'll assist in any way we can. Nash and I are driving over to the Best Beach Hotel right now, but it's slow going. That's why I called you, to see if you wanted in on this."

"I'm tied up all morning and probably this afternoon. I should wrap things up on the financial angle and then go see someone." He looked at his watch again. Time was flying. "Listen. I'll call you back when I know how the morning goes. I've got to find out where the Venezuelans at the hotel went to."

"OK. I'll stay in touch too. Do you want me to come over there?" There was real concern in her voice. "You don't sound right. Can I help with anything?"

"No," he said. "Go catch some bad guys." He ended the call.

He stood up too quickly and felt squeamish. He threw money on the table and slinked out of the dining room toward the front desk. He passed the bathroom and decided he had better get some water on his face. Then he rushed to the toilet and puked up breakfast. Twice, but he felt better. Catharsis.

He cleaned up and walked over to the front desk clerk.

"Good morning, Mr. Wilson. How can I help you?"

"I wondered if you've seen the Venezuelan conference people." *Not very subtle,* he thought. "I wanted to ask them some questions, if you know where they are. In the conference room?"

"Oh no. You have just missed the last of them. They left a short while ago. All of them."

"Where did they go?" His confusion was obvious.

"The airport, I think. But it isn't open yet, so I'm not sure."

"Just now?" Wilson was stunned again. "All of them?"

"Yes. A van picked them up."

"Do you know which company?"

"I don't know."

He felt at a dead end. A little desperate. "Thanks."

Wilson walked to Tim Martin's room and knocked on the door. Martin scowled at him.

"Where have you been? Did you hear back from your source yet?" Martin noticed Wilson's face, which was greenish in hue. "You OK, buddy?"

"I was delayed," Wilson said, struggling to the side table to set up his computer. "I'll check now."

He logged on and saw three emails from Langley. He opened the first one and read it. "What the hell?"

"What is it? Anything we can use?" Martin read over Wilson's shoulder.

Wilson moved his body to cover the computer screen. "Hey! It's my confidential source. No peeking. Let me parse it first. Then you can see."

It took a few minutes to absorb. Maybe he needed more coffee. He thought about what he could tell Martin. He rewrote it in simpler form, excluding all references to sources and methods. He made it bare bones. Martin waited on the edge of the bed.

"OK, here it is. Grenada Construction Company is a newly formed company in the last year. It was created when Wong first won the contract here. It's owned by a Venezuelan company named Marzo Adelante, or March Forward in English. They sent the money to Grenada Construction through an Aruba bank. It appears they're a unique company that handles only Chinese construction projects in Caracas. Most of their money comes from Chinese sources. I can't tell you how I got this or any of the details. It's classified. We'll attribute it to a confidential source in the banking industry."

"Holy shit!" Martin jumped up. "Who's your source? The Treasury Department?"

"I can't say. But it's as solid as it comes."

"Holy shit, holy shit!"

"There's more. Melbourne Consulting is a shell company for a very nasty outfit. If you go back along the routing of the money, it comes indirectly from World Electrosystems LTD, a subsidiary of Zangchung Industries in China. I think they're owned by the Chinese government, at least in part."

"Holy shit! Are you kidding? Are you crazy?" Martin was overjoyed at the news. Then he stopped and stared at Wilson. His eyes narrowed and his jaw dropped. "You're not shittin' me, are you? Is this real?" He got close to Wilson to study his face.

"Real as it can be. But what? Didn't you think the Chinese might be involved?" Wilson asked. "The talk all over town is that there's Chinese money funding the GPC campaign."

"Yeah, but rumor is one thing. Proving it is another. We gotta talk about your source, Robert. How reliable is it? I mean, if we're writing this, we better be damn sure it's right."

Wilson's head hurt again. "OK. Let's do this. We'll write the article and send it to your editor for verification. Your facts team can test it and see if they can back it up. If they come up with another source, we can include it and strengthen the article."

"Yeah, that sounds good. But it will burn a lot of time. We won't get this out today."

"Yeah, I know we won't get the Election Day explosion, but we'll still have dynamite."

Martin grinned from ear to ear. "OK. Let's do it."

"You get started. I have to check on a few other things." Wilson read two more emails, both confirming information about the Russian oligarch Boris Lavanenko. His relationship with Petrov was as expected, an insider who the premier trusted and someone who undertook certain missions for his ruler. He had his fingers in many Russian companies, from travel to electronics to military hardware. He was a major player.

Lavanenko! Wilson remembered he was meeting Pendergast by noon. It was already eleven.

He jumped up and immediately regretted the sudden movement. He pushed Martin from the chair where his computer was located and took over the writing task. "Sorry, Tim. I know just how we write this up. Let me do the draft, OK?"

Martin was upset but didn't argue. He stood by Wilson's side and read over his shoulder as his feverishly typed the story.

It just came to him, and he typed like a madman. In thirty minutes, he had finished the draft article. He reread it and then read it out loud to Martin. "What do you think?"

"Hell, that's great. Let me add a couple of things and then we can polish it up. Good goin'."

"Listen, Tim. I have a few things I have to take care of. Can I step out awhile and catch up with you in a couple of hours?"

"Yeah, sure. Or I can email you the final and you can comment over the phone."

"That works too." Wilson left the room, feeling like he had accomplished something important. If only his head would stop throbbing.

Chapter 16

Tuesday

Wilson was lying on his back on the wooden dock at Reefer Scuba Diving Adventures, the sea sloshing all around him and waves crashing on the end of the timber structure. Drizzle caressed his face. He was recovering from Pendergast's homemade hangover remedy. He had been assured that it would cure him in minutes, and it had been fast acting. He had sipped the smelly concoction, drinking only half before Pendergast suggested he step outside and not fall in the water. He had been violently ill for about three minutes and then a calm came over him as he realized he had survived the ordeal. His blood pressure was returning to normal, and his headache was dissipating remarkably well.

"Ya gonna make it?" Wet Dog checked on his condition by calling out from the office doorway.

"Yeah, I think. Maybe. Give me a minute." His voice seemed modulated somehow, but talking didn't hurt any longer. He rolled onto his side and felt like he might live. He sat up; not so good.

Wet Dog handed him a Stag. "This helps stabilize your brain."

Wilson took a sip of beer, and the tightness in his head began to recede. He sipped more and felt better. In a few minutes, he stood and did not sway. The mist on his face turned to moderate rain, so he shuffled back to the office. He sat on a chair and stared at Pendergast, who was grinning from ear to ear.

"Give it another ten minutes and you'll wonder what all the trouble was."

"It's getting better. That shit really works." He tried to grin, but it still hurt his eyes a bit.

"In the meantime," Pendergast said, "I have info on the *Shanghai Maiden,* your freighter. They didn't sail away, just into the harbor this morning to offload twelve containers. Put them directly on trucks that went to Wong's job site."

"What the hell?"

"Now on the Russians, news is that they're finishing up whatever they're doing out there. One of my men went out there fishing." Pendergast winked. "He saw them diving and also hauling some equipment onto the *Varoushka.* Not sure what the gear was, but it wasn't the usual stuff you need for treasure hunting." Pendergast seemed puzzled.

"What are they doing down there?"

"Down below, I couldn't tell ya. But I think they've been repairing something. Maybe a diving station underwater. They brought up a sort of diving bell. But we couldn't get close enough to see exactly what it was. Not anything we've seen before."

"What do they have down there?"

"If I knew that, I'd be a happy man."

"So that's it. That's why I'm here?"

"No. I'm offering my services as a diving consultant to help you figure out what they've been doing. Whenever they clear the area."

"Aren't we paying you now? For services rendered?"

"Yes, but this would be something new. Deep-water stuff, not just information gathering and driving a boat around." Pendergast looked quite earnest about it. "It would take special gases and a lot of time underwater, so it would add up. Could be dangerous too."

Wilson understood that the mystery was driving both him and Pendergast crazy. Could he get the funding for further investigation? "Get me a cost estimate, and I'll see where we can go from there. But keep on the other work, OK?"

"Will do. You feeling better now?"

"After that misery, I'm surprised to say I am." He walked out the door to the truck.

***

Wilson returned to the hotel via Grand Anse Road, which was flooded but did not seem any worse than it had since the previous day. Leslie was busy at the front gate, checking in cars and two vans. Wilson asked what was happening.

"We're receiving guests from another hotel down the coast, the Eldorado," Leslie said while writing on a clipboard. "Their seawall gave way in the night and most of their grounds were flooded. They evacuated all their first-floor people over to us, now that we have rooms available."

"Are there any other free rooms on the island now?" Wilson asked, curious. "I assumed every room was full by now."

"You're right, Mr. Wilson. There aren't any rooms left; everybody full up."

"So where did the Venezuelans move to this morning if there are no other rooms and no one can leave Grenada?"

"That be a good question and a half."

Wilson parked the truck and waded over to the main building, then he climbed the stairs to Martin's room on the second floor. He had finally stopped to buy a pair of waterproof Wellington boots at the mall. He bought the last ones in his size, settling for the orange tiger striped ones because that was all that was left. But his feet were dry.

"Wilson, thank God!" Martin greeted him by waving pages of text in his face. "Here is the final draft. If it looks good to you, we can send it off. We're running out of time."

Wilson took the pages and began reading their story. "Hey, this reads pretty well." He sat down and focused on the text. "Tim, have you eaten lunch yet? I'm starved."

"No. I was going down to eat a sandwich or something. Bring that and you can read while you eat."

They sat at a table and munched on breaded and pan-fried mahi-mahi fish and chips while Wilson read and made minor edits. When they finished eating, they had a final version ready for Martin's editor. Martin rushed off to submit the story and Wilson called Madeline.

"Robert, we have a problem. We got the arrest warrants by noon and then drove over to the Best Beach Hotel to make arrests. But the Venezuelans had moved out this morning. Some vans came and picked them up, all their luggage too. We don't know where they went."

"Same here. The remaining ones checked out this morning. No one knows where they went to, and there are no spare hotel rooms anywhere."

"The police are going through the rooms they were in, looking for anything that would indicate where they might be. No luck so far." She paused, a thoughtful silence. "It's like they just vaporized."

"Where are you now?"

"At the Best Beach, but I can leave."

"Why don't you meet me at the warehouse in a little while and I'll wrap up here. We got our story written about the foreign money. I'll bring you a copy."

"Good. I'll tell Lightchurch. He'll want to read it."

Wilson hung up and left the restaurant. He walked up to his room and checked whether anyone besides the maid had been there. He had already sanitized it as far as his agency work went, but he wanted to find that damn camera that Cortez had placed there to spy on him.

He began with the likely places where a camera could be hidden. Because a camera needed visual access, it was probably in a light fixture, an air vent, or a piece of furniture. He eliminated the vents and lights quickly by disassembling them with no results. Then he looked for any location that might seclude a micro lens. Again no result. Then he settled on the television set. It was more sophisticated than most setups, but it was plausible.

Most modern televisions were designed so that the speakers could function as microphones and pick up sounds in a room. This was partly because manufacturers had planned for the TVs to be interactive before the advent of Alexa and similar home-control devices. Given the right software, the TV could become a listening device. Some TVs had small cameras built into them, just as most laptops have a camera that could be switched on remotely. The beauty of using a TV for eavesdropping is that every hotel room had one, usually placed with a view of the room and thus any activities that occur.

He unplugged the TV and searched for any signs of tampering, finding only minor scratching on the back panel. He decided this was the likely surveillance device. He unhooked it from the wall and placed the TV in the closet with a blanket over the screen. The problem with this analysis was that the recorded video might have been transmitted over the cable wire and not broadcast by a transmitter. *Oh shit!*

That meant that the night he spent with Vargas might not have been scuttled by the jamming device he had employed. They had not spoken about anything incriminating when they were in the room that night, but their conversation and other antics may have been recorded anyway. Troubling.

The obvious place for a recording device was in the central communication room where the cable feed originated. The Venezuelans would have had access to it when they set up for their conference. Wilson would follow up on that later. Maybe he could find the copies of any videos made of him and Vargas. Maybe Gordon could help him with that. But Cortez probably already had the recordings. What would he do with them?

***

He said goodbye to Martin and then headed to the warehouse during a break in the storm. Madeline had already arrived and was working on her computer.

"Lightchurch will be here shortly," she said. She looked tired; her features were drawn and she didn't have her usual level of energy. "He was talking to the PM again this afternoon and said he'd have some good info for us when he gets here."

"OK. I'll give you both a sitrep then."

"So, Robert. This woman really got to you." Madeline stood up and walked to his side. She put a hand on his shoulder and gazed into his face before he turned away. "You care too much. It's unprofessional," she said stiffly. When she saw his reaction, she softened. "I'm sorry. I guess she got to you."

"She's just a nice woman, that's all. Let's not talk about it." He stepped away.

Just then Lightchurch arrived with two bodyguards. His face was set as if he were already making a decision that was distasteful.

"I just came from a meeting with the PM and the chief of the Royal Grenada Police Force. Before the meeting, the PM assured me that the chief was completely trustworthy and that we can share any information with him. He has a security clearance that is high enough for our work." He paced back and forth as he spoke. "I told them both about what you found at the Wong site and about the hidden men at the sports facility. They were shocked on both counts. They want to know more about these people, the Venezuelans, and what they're up to."

"That's good news, Sir," Madeline commented. "Do they want a detailed briefing?"

"I gave them all the news they could handle for now. The PM is still driven by the election, and the chief is preoccupied with providing security at all the polling stations. He said he cannot spare us more men until the polls close at six p.m."

"That's another four hours," Wilson said. "A lot can happen in that time."

"In the meantime, he wants us to take the chief and his men from the Best Beach Hotel up to the Wong site and have us show him where you saw all this hardware. The PM said he wanted the information verified by the chief before he could proceed."

"That's great news, Sir. When?"

"He'll call."

Wilson's cell phone pinged that an email had arrived, so he stepped aside. He read it first on the phone and then rushed to the laptop and read it again, printing out copies for the others. It concerned the voting machines.

The model 156-B Votadigit series was widely used in several countries, but there were some concerns about the storage capability of the machines. They stored the images of the ballots, but there were several instances where some ballots were lost due to insufficient memory in the devices. The model 156-B was an upgrade that linked the machine directly to the company's digital cloud for storage in a secure and encrypted form. No images were stored on-site, so the computers required less memory, making the machines less expensive to produce. Even the processing of results was largely handled off-site. The only problem occurred in some remote polling stations that were not attached to high-speed internet for direct communication. Special arrangements were made for those situations.

Further reading was interesting. Votadigit had been acquired by Datawarific Solutions of Canada three years ago and Digimatrose Communications of Singapore then purchased that company last year. Digimatrose was now one of the many companies owned by World Electrosystems LTD, a subsidiary of Zangchung Industries.

He distributed the copies and let the others read it for themselves.

"Does this mean what I think it means?" Lightchurch asked. "That the company can manipulate the voting results?"

"I'm afraid so, Darius," Wilson said. "It means that all data are stored off-site on the company server somewhere and so are the backup images. There would be no way of verifying the results if the hard-copy ballots themselves were lost."

"So Votadigit could control—no, invent—the election results and no one would know the difference without the paper ballots. It's madness."

"And there's more." Wilson passed each of them a copy of the article on campaign funding. They read in silence for several minutes.

"My God!" said Lightchurch. He waved the document in the air as he spoke. "The Chinese are trying to buy the election and fabricate its results at the same time. This is outrageous!"

"But why would they do this?" Madeline asked. "Do they want to take over our country?"

Lightchurch responded, "China would like nothing better than to have a foothold in the Caribbean Sea, an anchor from which they could pedal their influence. They are doing this several places in the world already. Usually they work by giving economic aid to third-world countries, where a little extra money and special public works projects can make a government friendly to them. Djibouti is one such country. They helped them with projects and now have a military base there and can project influence throughout the region."

"And it's not just about commercial ties either. They'll project military strength and influence over shipping routes too," Wilson added. "But let me ask you, Darius. How did the Cubans take over the government of Grenada in 1983?"

"Aha. You've hit it right on the head, Robert."

"I can answer that," Madeline said. "In 1983, Bernard Coard, a member of the New Jewel Movement, overthrew the existing Marxist government of Maurice Bishop, a man who became ruler in an earlier coup in 1979. He was not elected, but some

Grenadians respected him for his intentions. He made the mistake of inviting the Cuban government to help him by supplying labor and money for public works, the airport, roads, and other things. He let a lot of Cubans into the country for work. Similar to what the Venezuelans are doing in their country now regarding Cubans, for instance. But he did not know the Cubans were plotting with Coard on the overthrow. Once the Cubans were all in country and in position, it was a simple coup d'état in which they killed Bishop and several ministers."

"The new government was very unstable, with infighting running rampant among the communist factions," Lightchurch added. "There were riots in the street and chaos reigned. There were about one thousand Americans in the country at the time, many here on the island attending the medical school, much as they are today. This all occurred shortly after the Iranians took American hostages and there was concern that Coard would take the hostages. President Reagan feared a repeat of the Iran hostage situation, so he led an international coalition that restored democracy and rescued the Americans. That action restored the government in 1983."

"So the instability and threat to Americans foretold their downfall. It was a hard coup that collapsed," Wilson said. "I see something similar happening here. Only this might be a sort of soft coup."

"Why do you say that?" asked Lightchurch.

"Suppose you could rig an election and install into power a group or political party that is sympathetic to your goals," Wilson said. "Once the election is over, your supporters have a democratic basis of legitimacy. If that government is stable and it continues essential services, and it maintains diplomatic relations with other countries, there's no threat to anyone. Except to those who you replaced. Things would go on as usual, at least for a while."

"And maybe you wouldn't threaten the Americans so as not to invite a reaction," Madeline said. "So that would be the soft coup—little violence, and, if there is, it is only directed at a few specific people."

"It's still a coup," said Lightchurch.

"But it's more like a change of CEO in a company," Wilson said. "The board votes one guy out and puts a new one in place. The company business goes on."

"But the shareholders select the board members," Madeline commented. "It's not the same."

"OK, OK. Maybe the boardroom is a bad example," Wilson said. "And in this case, why do they need weapons and men if they're doing this through subterfuge in the election?"

"In case they don't get the desired result in the election," Madeline said. "They then do a hard coup." She raised her eyebrows and turned to Lightchurch. "We must interfere with these voting machines somehow and make the election commission count the ballots the old-fashioned way."

"We have to stop the machines," Wilson said. "We need to cut them off from the internet and the company server."

Lightchurch was becoming agitated. He paced back and forth. "I can't believe this is happening. And the Chinese are behind it."

"And the Venezuelans, too, with a little Cuban support," Wilson said.

"So the damn Cubans get their hands on Grenada one way or another after thirty-five years." He shouted, "Those bastards! It's a lot to take in."

"Hey, they haven't got it yet. Let's come up with a plan." Wilson sat up, pulled a tablet to him, and wrote down some notes. "First, Darius, you must inform the PM that there is vote tampering going on as we speak. We have time to intercept the counting process because they do that at the end of the day. Maybe he can do something that will ensure that the paper ballots get more protection than usual."

"Second," Madeline said, "we can cut the internet cable at several of the biggest voting stations so that they can't upload data to the cloud. That's the only sure way to stop them. Then they must do a manual count of the ballots, or at least use the old counting machines."

"Jesus, Madeline," said Lightchurch. He stood back and gazed at her in amazement. "You're a real agent of chaos."

"Sir, this requires immediate and direct action. We can't fuck around." She was firm in her response, and resolve showed in her face. She didn't say *fuck* very often. It got their attention.

"We can't do it ourselves. We have other things we must do," Wilson said. "Maybe we can have the PM make the decision and then have the police incapacitate the machines or at least change the process by keeping it off the internet."

"I'll call the PM right now. This is an emergency." Lightchurch stepped away and got on the phone.

"Robert, we still have too many moving parts to this coup that I don't understand." Madeline's face was a puzzle of emotion.

"Like where did the Venezuelans go?" he said.

Madeline's phone beeped, and she picked up a call. "Yes, sir. He's on another call, but I'm sure that will be all right. We'll meet you there in fifteen minutes." She hung up.

"The police chief wants us—you and me—to meet him at the Wong Construction site. He'll bring three men and make a special request that he search the site. If the site manager refuses, he'll get a search warrant and return."

"He needs direction so that they look in the right places?" Wilson asked.

"Right."

Lightchurch ended his call and looked discouraged. "I'm using up my good graces with His Honor. He said he'll consider it but wants to know what we find out at the Wong site first. If there really are weapons there, it will move everything up a notch, and he may declare a national emergency. But he said he needs proof, not theories." He began swearing under his breath.

"Sir, we're going to the Wong site right now. You'd better come. You'll need the results right away."

"OK. I'll take my car and men along just in case there's an altercation. You two drive together."

***

They all left the warehouse and drove east along Morne Rouge Road to the site. When they arrived, there were two police cars and a black Mercedes already at the front gate to the construction site. Madeline pointed out the chief of police, the highest-ranking law enforcement officer on the island. He was talking to two people, a Chinese man called Fu and the Grenada representative of Wong Construction, a man named Garland. None of them looked happy.

The chief was a tall, older gentleman with thinning white hair and a stern look that may have come from years of dealing with criminals and politicians. He dispensed with formalities as he began the meeting.

"Gentlemen, we're here to tour your construction site. We have had reports of the possible storage of weapons on your property and must determine if this is true. With your permission, we will walk the property with one of your men and see what we shall see."

"I resent your insinuation, sir," said the Chinese man, Fu. "It is insulting for you to come here."

Garland saw that this was the wrong thing to say to any police chief, and he tried to smooth out the answer. "What Mr. Fu means is that he finds it unreasonable that you should arrive at his construction site without warning or making an appointment. He left a very important meeting to talk to you, and he is upset that he has not been shown the correct level of respect that he deserves."

The chief looked at Fu and was about to say something, but he hesitated when his assistant whispered something in his ear. "I apologize, Mr. Fu." He gave a perfunctory dip of his head. "I'm sorry for the short notice and my failure to make proper arrangements for this inspection. But there are extenuating circumstances that have led me here so abruptly."

Garland conferred with Fu, and he seemed somewhat appeased. "Mr. Fu wishes you and your men welcome to his site office for normal procedure of tea and preliminary conversation." He acted as though this was a usual occurrence. "You see, gentlemen, Mr. Fu must contact his home office for their guidance for such a sudden invasion of the workspace. It is quite natural for the Chinese to require this approval, even though it may seem strange to us here in Grenada."

"Only for a few minutes, Mr. Fu, Mr. Garland. Then we will have the inspection to which we are entitled per your contract for operation in this country." The chief was clear.

They walked slowly to a nearby trailer that the construction company used as their field office. Fu urged all of them to sit while an assistant prepared green tea. They made small talk until the tea was ready, a ten-minute period of limited conversation. The chief tried to bring up the purpose for the inspection several times, but Fu or Garland always changed the direction of the conversation. Finally, Fu stood up and excused himself to take a phone call, presumably the call from his masters. He was gone for ten minutes.

"Mr. Garland, we can wait no longer." The chief stood up, and he and his people began walking toward the door.

That was when Mr. Fu returned and said that his home office had cleared everything. Mr. Garland was volunteered as their guide around the site in one of the company vans.

"No, Mr. Fu, we will drive ourselves on our inspection." The chief walked to his car, his driver leading the way.

Mr. Fu shouted something in Mandarin. Suddenly three Chinese guards holding AK-74 rifles blocked the chief's path. They raised their weapons. They were unsure of what Fu had said, but it was clearly unfriendly. Garland seemed as shocked as the Grenadians by this action. The chief's driver put his hand on his gun under his jacket. So did the two protective agents for Lightchurch who closed in around him and pulled out their weapons.

"Fu, you can't do this," the chief yelled.

Fu shouted again in Mandarin and more guards approached, their weapons held low. Garland said, "Mr. Fu insists that you ride in a company vehicle because it is required by our insurance company."

"Mr. Fu, Mr. Garland, any further attempts to delay our inspection will be dealt with in the most severe manner. Everyone on this property will be immediately arrested, including both of you. The site will be closed for months as we investigate what you are up to, and your contract will be canceled and awarded to a company that will cooperate with this nation."

Fu took a deep breath as he prepared to respond, but Garland held up his hand for him to hold his tongue.

The chief had a full head of steam up, and he glared at Fu. He took on a mean look. "No doubt Mr. Fu's employers will dismiss him as manager of this project, and he will likely not find work in any legitimate firm in the West or the East. And of immediate consequence, I will order my men to shoot the two of you directly upon the discharge of any weapon tonight."

The chief then turned to his men, who took aim on the two managers immediately. Eight men pulled their weapons slowly and aimed them at Fu and Garland.

Garland practically shit his pants. He started arguing with Fu in Mandarin, and the effect was dramatic. All the guards appeared nervous and looked to Fu for instructions. He seemed ready for a game of chicken, but Garland ordered the men to drop their weapons.

It was a Mexican standoff for about thirty seconds. Finally, Fu backed down and suddenly was all smiles. He apologized for a misunderstanding. Of course agents of the hosting government were exempted from the insurance conditions. *What a load of bullshit!* Wilson thought.

The chief waved everyone into their vehicles. Madeline took the lead and raced forward in her Land Rover toward the heart of the site. The chief insisted that Garland ride with him and show them the way. Five cars and trucks sped into the job site.

"I know that Mr. Fu was trying to delay our inspection and you were his accomplice. You had better hope that you can appease me with your full and complete cooperation now. Or there will be consequences, Mr. Garland. Do you understand?"

"Yes, sir. But he is my boss. I had to support him in this. Don't you see that?" Garland literally squirmed on the car seat as he spoke, like a worm on a hook.

"That will be your comfort while wasting away in prison, Mr. Garland."

Garland gagged, and it seemed like he was choking. Then he went silent. Madeline's choice of routes led to a dead end, and one of the chief's men poked Garland in the back with a finger, gaining his attention. They needed him to show them the way to the rear of the site. Garland jumped as if they had put a gun to his back. The man did as he was told, but his gray face looked as if his life had already been taken from him.

The road led past the current working area and to the back of the site. All five vehicles pulled up along the rear fence of the site and next to the same collection of containers that Madeline and Wilson had opened two days before. Everyone disembarked and walked to the first container, whose doors were unlocked. Wilson stepped forward and swung the doors open for all to see.

The container was empty.

He stepped to the next one and opened the doors. Also empty. Madeline and one of the police officers then ran to each of the containers and threw open the doors. All the containers were devoid of any contents whatsoever. Madeline set about taking photos of the containers as they stood there in some disarray.

Wilson eyed Garland, and he saw a sneer on the man's face. Apparently his boss's delaying tactics had paid off. They had been played.

Wilson was ready to choke the little weasel, but he controlled himself. "Let's check the warehouse next," Wilson said.

The entourage moved over to the warehouse just before darkness settled on the landscape. When they opened the doors of that building, they encountered little of interest. It had been emptied as well, except for a few cots, tools, and a flatbed, two-ton truck. They walked around the warehouse and the area where the containers had been stored. They found that there were fresh tire tracks and skid marks all around the containers. They also found a few rifle cartridges, 5.45×39mm, the caliber used in AK-74 assault rifles. Garland said they had several of those weapons on-site for security purposes.

There was little they could do, unless they searched every container on the site, and that would take time and likely yield the same result. Apparently, someone had either tipped the Wong people off or they had already moved the military equipment on their own schedule earlier. That thought made Wilson nervous. He caught Madeline's eye. "We've been fucked over."

The vehicles exited the construction site and pulled up in echelon on the side of the road just outside. They stepped out of the vehicles, and the chief assembled his entourage in a circle to say a few words.

"I am very embarrassed that we inspected that site and found none of the weapons that you two people reported." He looked sternly at Wilson and Madeline. "But I believe these weapons were there. They clearly were delaying us, and there can be only one reason for that. Or if there were no weapons, they had other illegal activities they were covering up. Either way, there is criminal activity going on here." He stared at each person in the circle. "I want each of you to know that I will not let this sort of activity continue in this country. But now I must report to the prime minister what we have not found and what we have found."

One of the policemen asked, "What do you mean, Chief? We found nothing. The raid was a complete failure."

The chief smiled and laughed gently. "No, my friend. We have found out about a conspiracy, and we found this." He held up one of the rifle cartridges they had found on the ground. He passed it to the policeman for examination.

"Sir, this is an armor-piercing round. This is strictly regulated ammunition."

"Yes, it is illegal to possess this in this country. Our inspection was not a failure. We now have evidence of illegal activity and a strong basis for a warrant to shut the entire site down for further investigation." He chuckled loudly, but then his face hardened dramatically. "No one plays the fool on me. No one."

He looked directly at Wilson. "No one."

Chapter 17

Tuesday

During the evening, Tropical Storm Betty made landfall and kicked up the storm surge again with high winds but less rain than before. The wind wreaked havoc on the entire island, blowing down trees and power lines, creating whitecaps on the sea, and lashing everything exposed with harsh rain and flying debris. Telephone lines and TV cable transmissions were interrupted completely or made extremely unreliable. But still, the dedicated voters of Grenada turned out in record numbers to do their duty and exercise their right to select their own leaders.

The power went out at the Hempstead, and the new generator kicked in, maintaining emergency levels of power. All rooms still had water and lights, but television and phone service were curtailed. Power was routed to all refrigeration equipment in the kitchen and food storage areas to keep food from spoiling, but there wasn't enough power for the air conditioners or for the refrigerators in individual rooms. Guests could take their perishable goods to the restaurant where the hotel pledged to place food in cool storage for their guests. No one needed air-conditioning anyway with the horrific winds blowing across the property. Only the main bar and restaurant remained operating.

Wilson, Madeline, and Martin sat at a table near the bar and sipped Carib beers that were partly cool. They were waiting for word on how they should proceed in each of their endeavors. Martin waited for a call back from his editor about the election-funding article, spending the time cribbing notes about a second article he had started about the storm and its effect on the election. Madeline waited to hear back from the chief on whether he had obtained a search warrant for the construction site. Wilson wondered what would happen next on all fronts—the freighter, the missing weapons, the Chinese construction site, Tori Vargas, and the bloody Russians—what were they up to? They were all upset or on edge as they dwelled on their own private worries.

Then it hit him. "The sports facility. Maddie we better check on the sports facility. Are those people still there?" He jumped to his feet. "We have to go."

Madeline jumped up too. "You're right. In all this other mess, I had forgotten about that place."

"What are you guys talking about?" Martin asked. "What sports facility?"

"We'll tell you later." Wilson was already at the door, with Madeline right behind.

They splashed through a foot of seawater to the truck and drove out of the car park. Wind was whipping the palm trees over their heads and bits of vegetation flew through the air. Occasionally, a piece of wood or metal roofing, torn loose from a building, whipped over their vehicle. There was very little traffic on the road except for people with tall vehicles, high-clearance ones. Most people had reverted to wading to wherever they needed to be.

A column of three police vehicles full of men in uniform crossed their path heading downtown. Madeline looked at them. "They must be new vehicles because the police always use olive-green Land Rovers for patrols, not Toyota Land Cruisers."

They arrived at the sports facility to find the lights off and the parking lot empty of vehicles, unlike the last time they had been there. They got out of the truck quietly and approached the front door with caution. No one appeared to be around. That seemed unlikely on a day when most people would retreat to shelter. The front door was locked, so they fought the wind to the rear door. It was also locked, but its window was not blocked out like the others and they could see inside.

There was no one there. They tried the large garage door and found it unlocked. Wilson lifted the door while Madeline held her pistol at the ready.

An empty building. Wilson was getting tired of finding nothing where he knew there had been something only days before. They entered and then slammed down the door, shutting out the fierce wind.

It was very dark inside with all the windows blocked with either cloth or cardboard. The lights didn't work either because of the storm. There was little they could do except confirm that the place had been abandoned and largely cleared out except for several boxes and many pieces of luggage stacked along the wall.

"Now we have another hundred men unaccounted for. Where the hell are they?" Wilson complained.

"There's not much we can do here. We'll inform the chief, and he can get a search warrant to go through these things that they left behind." Madeline was apoplectic about their findings. "Maybe they'll come back for something." She kicked one of the cots that stood idly by on the floor.

"OK. Let's head for the warehouse and catch up with Lightchurch." Wilson was shocked that they found nothing there. The Venezuelans, Cubans, and Chinese were always one step ahead of them. They had to catch up with the game.

***

They drove to the warehouse through flooded streets. They were suddenly cut off at the Mourn Rouge roundabout by a convoy of six police vehicles, driving fast and headed toward the downtown area.

"More Toyotas. I didn't know they were upgrading the police fleet." Madeline's voice was doubtful.

The radio in the truck blared out a news report that evacuations of residents along the northwest coast would begin in the morning. The volcano had sent out a vast belch of sulfurous smoke, and minor earthquakes signaled a greater eruption in the offing.

"That's all we need now," said Wilson. "A major eruption and a tidal wave."

At the warehouse, they encountered Lightchurch and his security people. He was on the phone when they entered.

"But, sir!" he shouted into the phone. "You must decide now because once the polls close, they will begin the counting process. It will be too late in an hour . . . I *know* it is unprecedented." He held the phone to his ear and waved Madeline over. He put his hand over the speaker and said to her softly, "I hope you have some wire cutters. I don't think he'll make the decision."

"Sir, the polls should have closed by now. It may be too late," Madeline said. "Let me make a few calls to see what's happening." She retreated to the far side of the room to use her cell phone, which was still working in spite of the weather.

Wilson waited for something to happen. He attempted to put it all together in his mind. *Where had everyone gone to? Why had they suddenly disappeared? And where were the weapons?*

Then it hit him. He jumped up and shouted, "They've already deployed! That's why we can't find anyone." He rushed over to Madeline and grabbed her arm. "The police we saw on the road must be impostors. Nearly all the police should still be guarding the polling stations or out helping stranded people. They wouldn't be driving around in convoys. That's why they were driving Toyota Land Cruisers, not Land Rovers."

Madeline's eyes registered what he implied. She ended her call and turned to him, excitement in her eyes. "You're right, Robert. I knew there was something odd about those police vehicles. Where were they going?"

"I don't know. That's the problem." He looked puzzled, then turned to her again. "What did you find out about the voting?"

"I called a friend who works as a volunteer at the polling station in south Saint George's. She said they lost power for a while and still can't reestablish their internet connection. She said that has happened at three other stations, and they may forget the new computers and revert to offline counting. If they do that, they can't save the images of the ballots and would have to consolidate the results from each station by hand. Some of the remote stations won't be able to bring in physical ballots for storage until the storm passes anyway."

"So maybe Tropical Storm Betty saved the day. That's great."

"I must tell Lightchurch so that he can inform the PM." She stepped away to talk to Lightchurch, who asked the PM to hold. After another minute, he ended his call.

"Thank God that's settled," Lightchurch said loudly, exasperated. "The man is overwhelmed with all these issues happening. I can't say as I blame him. It's a lot to process." He turned to Madeline. "What else aren't you telling me? I could use some good news."

"Well, Sir, we think there may be people impersonating policemen and driving in Toyotas that are painted to look like normal police patrol cars. We saw several vehicles traveling in a convoy toward the city center a short time ago."

"I asked for good news."

"We also drove by the sports facility and found out those men are now gone as well. If you count them, the missing Venezuelans, and the Chinese we saw at the construction site a few days ago, that makes close to three hundred men we can't account for," Wilson added.

Lightchurch looked devastated. "Jesus Christ. This is a disaster!" he shouted to no one in particular. He threw some papers across the room. He stood up and walked to the side counter where he kept an ample supply of whiskey— Glenmorangie, his favorite. He poured three fingers into a glass and walked back to his place at the table. He signaled the others to join him with a glass if they wished. They all shook their heads. They were on duty and would likely be involved in gunplay before long, the way things were sorting out.

"I cannot call the chief or the PM and give either of them more bad news without a plan, something proactive that will solve these mysteries." He seemed despondent for a few moments. "Come on, everyone. What are they doing? What's their plan?" He shook his hands in the air in frustration.

"Well, Sir, let's look at it from their point of view, shall we." Madeline spoke up, seemingly very calm. "Suppose Robert was right and they planned a soft coup. They would wait for the election results, which would come in around nine p.m., and they could wait for that before doing anything. Normally, the results would be announced on television and the new PM would say a few words."

"In that case, they wouldn't need to mobilize for several days because it would take a while for the new government to get organized, right?" Wilson said. "If their side won the election, they wouldn't do much, just stand by and gradually take over different ministries."

"Yes, starting with the police force and coast guard, I would suppose," Lightchurch mused.

"But what if something went wrong?" Madeline said. "Then they might change their plan."

Wilson began pacing the floor, as he did in times of stress. "Suppose something happened that interfered with the plan. Like someone finding out they had military equipment in hiding and ready for use. Or the voting scenario looked like it would fall through. Then what would they do?"

"They may have moved up the timetable. Go to a hard coup!" Lightchurch shouted. "Then we're back where the Cubans were thirty-five years ago." He sprang up from his chair and held his arms in front of him as if he were looking at some dire scenario from the future.

Nash interrupted. "Sir, I've just received a call that the national television service and the radio stations have all gone off the air."

"So it's started," said Lightchurch. He stood next to the table and looked them each in the eye.

"We don't have a standing army that can counter a takeover," Madeline said. "We have about sixty people in the coast guard and about nine hundred police, but they're scattered all over the island. Most of them don't carry weapons."

"I'll contact the chief and the PM. They need to know what's happening." Lightchurch's phone beeped. "Ah, that's the chief now."

Wilson and Madeline continued brainstorming while Lightchurch made his desperate phone calls.

"The obvious things they would do are to cut communications," Wilson said. "Take over the airport and shipping, then occupy government offices and banks. Later, they may take foreign personnel for hostages. That seems like the terrorist playbook," Wilson said.

"We had better arm ourselves for a fight. There are extra weapons here in the vault." Madeline led the others to the storage vault, where they all selected automatic weapons and ammunition. Lightchurch's guards, Morgan and Mitchell, each took assault rifles and extra ammo. Then Madeline shouted, "My God! We have rocket-propelled grenades back here and other hardware."

Lightchurch finished his conversation with the chief of police and joined them at the vault. "When I had this facility established, I had to plan for all eventualities, including another invasion." Lightchurch chuckled. "Of course, those weapons are for our own self-defense, mind you."

Lightchurch called for their attention. "The chief said they're coming under fire at the main gate to the government houses in the botanical gardens complex. He has a few well-armed men there, but he needs more time to get the rest of his forces organized. His people are in the process of notifying all departments and all his police stations. He feels that his men can defend the stations well as long as they're attacked by relatively small forces. They're much better prepared than they were during the last invasion."

"What can we do to help?" asked Nash.

"The chief asked if we could act as a relief force at the government offices," Lightchurch said. "We could engage the attackers from behind as they carry out their assault. He said he'll send down one man who will coordinate with us. Meet him at the roundabout." He paused. "Sounds like a valuable idea. We can give them support until they assemble."

***

Darkness had fallen by that time, and rain fell in intermittent squalls. The wind was still up, but somehow Wilson had the impression that the storm was receding. He hoped the rain didn't continue all night. It was getting old, and he, like the others, felt soaked through to the skin most of the time.

They loaded all their weapons into the three vehicles they had available and drove along the main road toward downtown, which took them past the government complex. The road that led to the offices turned off the central roundabout on Paddock Road and encountered a gate within forty yards. They saw two Toyota Land Cruisers blocking the entry. They pulled over just past the entry road, and a man waved them down.

"I'm Jeffers. The chief sent me." Madeline recognized Jeffers as one of the men with them at Wong's that afternoon. "They have about twelve men at the gate in police uniforms. The uniforms are not like ours. They have an extra flag on their shoulders, but the flags are sewn on upside down. So you can tell us apart if you have binoculars or meet them up close. I have men on the far side, but they will now pull back so that we can shoot." He talked on a handheld radio.

Jeffers, Nash, and Madeline led the assault, with Morgan on the right side of the road. Wilson and Mitchell stayed with Lightchurch as his bodyguards. The idea was that Morgan would draw fire to get the attention of the foreigners while the others would drop on them from the left, hopefully catching them off guard.

Theory is always superior to the way things unfold during combat. Almost immediately, Morgan came under heavy fire from the gate's defenders. He took cover and was hardly able to raise his head to return fire. As soon as the shooting began, Jeffers and the others laid into the gatehouse and dropped three men. Then they in turn came under fire and were pinned down. The flash and roar of automatic weapons fire cut through the dark scene.

The situation didn't look good as more men arrived in the fake uniforms. Wilson saw an opportunity and picked up one of their hand grenades and an H&K MP5 machine gun. He slipped away from the cars and made his way through some bushes on the left side of the gate where he had a shot at two of the foreign fighters. He pulled the pin on the grenade and stood up long enough to pitch it underhand toward the gate. He ducked down as someone fired at him. He waited three seconds for the blast. The gatehouse exploded in a fireball, and a few attackers crawled out of the small building. Then Wilson stood up and shot the men who were still armed and ready to fight. He retreated for cover.

Jeffers and the others moved in and killed four more men hiding behind the gatehouse itself. They saw three wounded men, and Jeffers radioed that the gate was open. He went about disarming the wounded and verifying the kills. Then he zip-tied the hands of the injured men who were still a threat. He and the others moved up the road and dislodged other foreign fighters. Wilson returned to the cars and stood guard. The fighting went on for thirty minutes while Lightchurch, Wilson, and Mitchell listened in on the radio. Finally, Jeffers and the others, along with additional police officers, walked down the road and reclaimed the gate. Six police with heavier weapons took over the defense of the government buildings. They still heard gunfire up the hill in the distance.

"Thanks for the help. You arrived at the right time to make a difference." Jeffers leaned down to talk to Lightchurch through the window of his car. "And thank you, Sir Lightchurch, for the warning. We had time to deploy automatic weapons because of your call. We had more firepower than they expected."

"How many men did they have?" asked Nash.

"Forty or fifty. There's a small group of ten or so who escaped up the hill, but they'll encounter a fence soon, and then we'll have them trapped." He saluted Lightchurch. "I had better get back with my men. We have at least three killed, several more wounded." He turned and jogged away toward the sound of the guns.

"Well," Madeline said appreciatively. "We don't have a standing army, but we certainly have some well-trained police. They're much better armed than they were thirty years ago. That's a good thing."

Wilson couldn't wait to ask, "Did you guys notice these were all Hispanic men, no Chinese?"

"I noticed that they were speaking Spanish to each other, yes. What does that mean?" Nash asked.

"It means the Cubans and Venezuelans took the lead on capturing the government offices here. I wonder where the Chinese guys are."

Madeline came over. "I was inspecting those bodies by the gate. None of them had IDs on them. They looked Latin to me, maybe Venezuelans." She looked at Wilson. "Why no ID?"

"Probably so that they can deny involvement if they're captured. The Russians did that in the Ukraine and Crimea. The little green men, remember? No proof that another country was involved."

Madeline shook her head. "This is becoming scary now."

They could hear the sounds of gunfire from two different parts of town, one of them very intense. A fire engine's siren screamed far away, near Grand Anse. Lights in several parts of town were out.

Two Toyota Land Cruisers rushed up around the circle and slid off onto the entry road toward the government offices. The drivers didn't seem to notice the three cars pulled over past the circle. One of the vehicles skidded to a halt and lined up with the guard station, or what was left of it. That Toyota had a .50-caliber machine gun mounted on its roof, with a cockpit chopped out behind the gun. A man stood up there and began firing at the policemen. The second Toyota disgorged a half-dozen men who spread out and attacked the gate.

Madeline was angry, even though her wounded side hurt like hell. "Damn it, we just did this." She reached in the back of the truck, grimaced, and pulled out one of the RPG launchers. Then she attached a rocket to it and stepped out for a clear shot at the machine gun. With no hesitation, she fired the RPG at the Toyota and watched it blow up in a fireball.

"Well done, my dear!" Lightchurch called out. Fighting continued, but the foreign fighters were routed quickly.

Lightchurch's phone beeped and he answered. After a few minutes, he ended the call and spoke to them all. "The police chief is coming down here with one man. He wants us to join him as he investigates the sports facility. He wants to make a quick in and out but doesn't want his men tied up. Because we're not officially allowed to enter combat, he's enlisted us as his bodyguards. He also thought we would be most interested."

***

When the chief's Land Rover appeared, they drove behind him to the facility. Once there, the chief warned them about tampering with possible evidence, but he had to know what the men had been doing there and who they were. That was the sole purpose of the trip.

They entered the building the same way Madeline and Wilson had before, through the large garage-like door at the rear. When it was clear that there was nobody there, they began marching around the interior, following the chief through the main room. They came to the boxes, and the chief donned plastic gloves as he examined the contents of four boxes. They contained uniforms that read *FAR-Cuba* on them, the Forces Armadas Revolucionarias.

"It looks like they would put these on when the coup was complete," said the chief. "You men can now look through any of these other bags and boxes. Report anything of interest." He started stalking along the line of boxes. "Open some of this luggage, but be careful for booby traps."

The final comment slowed things down considerably. Four people searched bags while three stood guard in case any of the missing men came back to the building.

After they had moved several pieces of luggage, Wilson saw one bag that looked familiar. It was the huge, square, green-flowered bag he had seen at the hotel.

"Hey! That's Tori Vargas's bag, I think." He walked to it and pulled it free of the other items. It was very heavy, and he became suspicious. He laid it on its side as Madeline approached to see what he had found. It was one of those big soft-sided suitcases with a zipper on three sides. He unzipped it and then got a bad feeling as something red dripped from one side of the zipper.

He stood up and froze. He couldn't continue.

"What's wrong?" asked Madeline. She saw his distress and then the blood that oozed from the bag. She took charge. "Let me do this, Robert." She leaned down and flipped open the cover of the suitcase.

"Holy Jesus!" She jumped back.

Inside the suitcase was the naked and contorted body of Tori Vargas, who had been roughly stuffed into the case. Her tortured body showed signs of burns from cigarettes and other red-hot objects. She was folded up into a more or less fetal position. Her head was wrapped in a plastic bag and showed considerable blood on its inside surface.

Wilson stared at his former lover. *Oh my God!* he thought. He felt sick and rushed for the door. He was overcome with revulsion. He stood outside in the drizzle and fresh air for fifteen minutes. He threw up everything he had eaten that day and had dry heaves for a while. He couldn't go back inside.

Madeline came outside to check on him. She treated him gently, placing an arm over his shoulder for comfort. They stood that way awhile. She said nothing. He would learn more details about Vargas's death soon enough. *What a way to die,* he thought.

After a few moments, Wilson said to Madeline in a calm voice, "Cortez did this. He tortured her, then killed her." He paused to see if she understood his fury. "I'll kill the bastard if I find him. I'll make him pay." She kept her arm around his shoulders to comfort him as his eyes welled up.

Nash asked them both to return inside with him. Lightchurch had found something. He was waiting at the other end of the room from Vargas's remains, which had been covered by a blanket. "We found that the uniforms have the names of the soldiers who had come here for this invasion. All these men are apparently Cuban soldiers. I'm betting they were under the command of your old friend, Major Cortez."

Wilson focused on the subject at hand. "So they're Cubans. That would explain a lot. How many?"

"Based on the uniforms, one hundred and eight. There were spare policemen's uniforms, too, so it looks like these men were our phony police in Toyotas."

"We saw a lot of Toyotas here the day we reconned the place."

Lightchurch's phone beeped, and he picked up the call. He spoke for a while and then disconnected. "Good news. The police have intercepted and killed several more foreigners at the election commission. They'll have the election results soon, after nine o'clock."

"Cubans?" asked Wilson.

"Yes. No Chinese have been seen yet. It sounds like the police are able to handle this conflict fairly well. I'm glad." Lightchurch looked at Wilson and Madeline. "Look, you two, there isn't anything more you can do for a while at least. This place will be shut down as a crime scene now. Why don't you take a couple of hours and get some rest. That's what I'm doing as soon as we finish here."

Madeline took Wilson's arm and tugged at him. "Come on. We can go to your hotel and eat or sit in the bar at least. Try to get your mind off her."

They drove their separate rides to the hotel. Wilson went to his room and changed into drier clothing. When he came down to the main bar, he found Madeline talking with Tim Martin, both sipping Stag beers. He joined them but drank water until his stomach settled down.

Martin realized that something bizarre had happened. At first he asked them a million questions, but seeing their faces and getting no answers, he tried to lighten the mood. He poked Wilson in the shoulder. "It looks good for publication tomorrow, but editorial is still screwing with it."

Madeline's phone rang and she answered. "Oh really? Well, I'm not surprised. The details will come in the morning . . . Great. Good night."

"What was that?" asked Martin.

"The election results are in. The National Standard Party won all the ministerial seats like last time. Senjai and the GPC lost all major contests. The commission will compile everything and have it ready for broadcast tomorrow or whenever the TV comes on again." She held up her fist and shrieked. Then she shouted out to everyone in the bar. "The NSP won all seats again. Woo-hoo!"

More than half the people in the bar cheered; the few who had voted otherwise seemed stunned. "I'll buy a round, guys. Make it a good one." Wilson ordered Glenlivet and a club sandwich. Martin ordered more beer.

They ate and drank for an hour. Wilson had two whiskeys and felt like he might survive the night. He tried to put Tori Vargas out of his mind. He couldn't think of her, or he knew he would lose control of his emotions. It all felt surreal to him. How could that be possible?

Wilson's phone beeped. It was Pendergast. "I thought you'd want to know that the *Shanghai Maiden* is back at anchor again near where it's been all along."

Wilson's head began hurting again. "How's that?"

"They offloaded some containers, then drove back and anchored. I don't know what they're doing."

"What the hell is with those guys? Don't they have any other business?"

"Beats me," Pendergast said. "Got other news you're goin' to like too. You ready?"

"Yeah, hit me."

"The *Varoushka* is nowhere to be seen. Seems like the Ruskies shipped out last night sometime."

"Oh man. You're a source of merriment for me at all times." Wilson contained his need to vent. He looked out the window, and sure enough, he could just make out the mooring lights of the black freighter, his nemesis.

"OK. I'll need to think about all this. Thanks." He hung up.

"What was that all about?" asked Madeline.

"I'm not feeling so good. Call me if there's anything important. Otherwise, I'll be sleeping." He didn't wait for a response. He walked out of the bar, his head spinning with too much news.

Chapter 18

Wednesday

Wednesday was dominated by the tail end of two storms. Tropical Storm Betty was finally ready to stop tormenting the island of Grenada. The winds lessened, the storm surge began falling, the rain slackened to scattered showers, and the lightning ceased driving thunder through the skies. The sun made a dramatic appearance late in the day, providing a rainbow as consolation for Betty's rude visitation.

The second storm was one made by men who chose to overturn years of peaceful existence on the land and pervert it for their own gain. That storm had raged through the night in battle after battle, the protectors of the peace fighting the well-armed foreign menace. It had been a struggle, but the tide had turned in favor of the islanders.

Fighting had continued all night at several locations, the most contentious of these battles being at the downtown government office building where foreigners had invaded the structure. It took a great effort before the police could dislodge the intruders who had figuratively dug in to defensive positions. The police fought bravely but made slow progress.

Several battles had gone well, some not so well for the police. They liberated the radio/TV station from the foreigners but had many casualties and lost a few hostages in the process. Fortunately, the intruders had knocked out the station's broadcast capability when they overran the station, denying themselves the fruits of their labor. By sunrise, the invaders still had two hostages who were their only remaining means of survival.

Of the seven locations that the foreigners had targeted, only the hospital, the central bank, and the airport remained in their control. Eight men held hostages at the hospital, and they had made demands for safe passage to the airport to rejoin their desperate brothers there. They had already harmed several patients in an attempt to prove their resolve. Negotiations continued.

The second-largest and most successful attack had been on the airport, where fully half of the Cuban forces had been deployed to obtain an aviation beachhead of sorts so that additional troops could be brought in for their support. Fighting there had been intense, partly because the better-trained Cuban army was led by their overall commander, Major Cortez. After skirmishes around the airport facility, twenty-two Cubans and thirty-six Grenadian police officers had perished, along with several airport employees and tourists. The number of active Cuban fighters had fallen to thirty-five, with some of those suffering serious injuries. Hostages were also part of the situation there. No negotiations were seriously under way, as the battle was still intense.

No attempt had been made to secure the harbor or any number of other transportation facilities. No one knew why the foreigners—the Cubans, Venezuelans, and Chinese—had failed in these efforts. Perhaps there had been a shortage of troops for those objectives. In any case, the harbor was not very active. Reports were that only one terminal was busy loading containers onto a single ship with great deliberation. The cranes and ship were manned entirely by Chinese staff.

After the storm, life at the Hempstead on Grand Anse Beach began with the staff busily providing services and the guests clamoring for breakfast in spite of the difficulties of the current conditions. Tim Martin was sipping his morning coffee when he learned that the election interference story he and Wilson had penned was posted in the online version of the *Miami Observer*. His story broke on the Caribbean world with great consternation that any country would interfere with the elections of another sovereign nation. He was getting calls from his editor to write more copy and to feed the sudden need for details of the ongoing revolution. Martin was one of the few journalists lucky enough to be right in the thick of things, an enviable spot for any writer.

The volcano had sent mild earthquake tremors throughout the island. No one knew what that meant. There was no news to keep people informed because the radio and TV stations were all off the air. The people at the bar speculated about possible eruptions and tidal waves. One man said he saw strange waves that might presage a tidal surge. That scared the hell out of everyone into at least ordering more drinks and thinking about which direction to run if a huge wave suddenly appeared in front of the resort.

Tim Martin and Wilson were two of the few journalists on the island who could cover the volcano story. Unless something dramatic happened, like a huge eruption and a massive wave sweeping over the island—then they might not be around to write any story. Martin settled in to drink rum punch and looked terrified with each new tremor. "I'll die in a temblor," he mumbled sadly. "Story of the century, and I'll just wash out to sea."

Robert Wilson awoke in his room later that morning with a headache, a mild hangover, and a sense of dread. His sleep had been plagued by horrendous dreams of a young woman being tortured to death and then unceremoniously crammed into a suitcase. The dream had come back throughout the night, never letting him forget his guilt in its origination. Even as he showered and tried to shake off the vestiges of the dream, it ran in the back of his mind.

He dressed and then threw open the drapes that cloaked his lair from daylight's intrusion. He stared out at the sea, now still rough, but not whitecapped, and reflecting some of the sky's blue patches. Waves crashed on shore, forming long lines of white surge as they moved diagonally to follow the length of the beach, only to do so again and again. Seagulls and pelicans were out again, signaling the end of the storm and hunting for fish after a long fast. The storm surge was gradually draining away from the land after so many days of flooding.

The black freighter was gone.

Shit! How could this happen to me again? It was his watch, and he had somehow failed his mission again. Where had the damn ship gone to this time?

He picked up his phone and was assaulted by its flat, dead battery. His lifeline had abandoned him. He grabbed his charger and ran out of the room in his bare feet to the main bar, where he plopped down on a stool and searched under the edge of the bar for the electrical outlet he had used once before to recharge his battery.

Gordon happened to be tending bar and brought him a cup of hot, black Grenada roast to start off his day. "Good morning, Mr. Wilson. It was a hell of a night, eh?"

Wilson wasn't sure if he meant that he had had nightmares, too, or if he read the depths of exhaustion and despair that must have haunted Wilson's features.

"A hell of a night, indeed." Mr. Morant sat down next to Wilson for a chat. "There's still fighting at the airport and at Government House, they say. My suppliers are still making their deliveries in spite of the uprising."

"Uprising? What do you mean?"

"I suppose some of the GPC people are upset that they lost the election yesterday and are trying insurrection as a means for success," Morant said. "We still have no radio or TV. The storm must have wiped them out, too, like so many services."

"But there was an attempted military takeover of the government last night!" Wilson shouted. "Cuban soldiers were involved."

"Oh, Mr. Wilson. You must have really tied one on last night." Morant seemed amused. "Cubans? Why, that was long ago. That couldn't happen in this day and age. Countries don't just invade other countries." Morant called over to someone and then excused himself as he dealt with a delivery.

"But it's true," Wilson said to no one in particular. Gordon brought him the bar menu, and he ordered. By this time, his cell phone had a minimal charge. He dialed Pendergast.

"She's in harbor now loading some containers on deck. Been there since sunup," Captain Jimmy said. "They must be in a hurry to sail out of here with all the talk of revolution going on. Say, what have you heard about the takeover? With no radio, we're just getting rumors. Some say it's just a few opposition guys letting off steam."

"I can't really say just now. I have to make some calls." He hung up.

He sat at the bar recharging his phone battery and his psyche while eating breakfast. He tried raising Lightchurch and Madeline with no luck. He wondered what had happened last night after he had turned in. Without TV, radio, and his computer for internet, there was no way to get an update. There was little communication going on anywhere on the island except for a few cell phones and no information coming into or leaving the country. Almost nobody knew what was going on, and what they did know was based on rumor.

Finally, his phone beeped. It was Madeline. "Where the hell have you been? I've been trying to reach you. Get your ass over to the warehouse." She hung up.

Wilson returned to his room and got what he needed for the day: phone, charger, handgun, and binos. Everything else was still at the warehouse. The nightmare had settled into the back of his conscious mind. He knew that the horrors would likely return when he lay down to sleep.

Chapter 19

Wednesday

He drove the truck over to the warehouse, water still filling the streets, and went inside to meet Madeline. Lightchurch was there, as were the same men who had fought at the government offices. They were in the middle of a discussion about the current fighting by the foreigners. Another mild earthquake shook the building.

"The chief said that the intruders at the airport are the main problem. They're well organized and equipped, although they do not have the heavy weaponry that Madeline and Robert reported seeing four days ago," Lightchurch said. "The questions, then, are where are those weapons, and where are the Chinese fighters we expected?"

"The fighters at the airport are Cubans too? No Chinese?" asked Wilson as he pulled a chair up to the table.

"So far, only Venezuelans and Cubans have been encountered. We were just discussing what this means," Nash said.

"Our assumption has been that elements from the three countries were involved in the coup. The arms used so far are of Chinese manufacture, even though the serial numbers have been removed from individual weapons," Lightchurch said.

"It seems odd to me," Wilson said. He directed his attention to Lightchurch. "I did hear from a source that there are no Cuban fighters at the harbor, which is one of the targets that we expected would be overrun. But my source said that there are Chinese workers at the port loading containers onto a ship, the *Shanghai Maiden*. No locals are helping."

Lightchurch stared at him in disbelief.

Madeline continued the weapons discussion. "Really? That seems strange. Maybe they didn't commit to the use of military force but still supplied the weapons? Why would they make such an arrangement?"

"Maybe the parties had a disagreement of some kind," Wilson said. "If that's the case, the foreigners were undermanned. But if they were not all in agreement, why would the Cubans and Venezuelans proceed with an understrength invasion force?"

"Perhaps the calculus changed when the Chinese learned that the soft coup wasn't going to work," Lightchurch said. "If they were involved in a military overthrow of a government in the Caribbean, maybe it would be bad for their business with other countries in the region. They might be more interested in spreading their business interests than in military expansion."

"That would be consistent with their longer-term view of dominating the world," Nash said.

"Well, so much for philosophy. What we must know now is where the rest of those weapons are." Lightchurch came back to the practical question at hand.

"Without a police escort, I doubt if we can get back onto the Wong property. That will have to wait," Madeline said.

"Wait a minute," Nash said. "If the Chinese decided to drop out of the coup, why give the other forces light arms but none of the heavy gear they would need for a complete takeover?"

Wilson quietly thought about the problem, as did the others. If the Chinese had moved the weapons into the country, they had control of them and apparently stored them at the Wong job site. The Cubans and Venezuelans apparently already had their small arms from the Chinese. They could distribute them easily to the sports facility where most of the men could be armed. But they couldn't disguise the larger weapons.

"Suppose we look at this from a timing point of view." Wilson began pacing the floor. "We know that the weapons were at the Wong site on Saturday night but were gone by Tuesday night. The Venezuelans left the hotels late Monday and early Tuesday. The Cubans had left the sports facility by Tuesday evening. So that means the small weapons were distributed Sunday or Monday. But the heavy stuff was kept under wraps until late Tuesday."

"That all makes sense, but so what?" asked Morgan.

"The coup was probably not supposed to start until after the election results were announced late Tuesday or early Wednesday. They may have planned to distribute gear on Tuesday night but not to do anything obvious until the next day or even later." Wilson continued with his scenario. "Suppose it became clear to the Chinese that the election was not going their way. They would have known that by Tuesday evening after they had distributed the lighter arms."

"What if something went wrong with the plan?" Madeline picked up on the analysis. "Suppose they decided it was not working out as planned and had second thoughts. They may have wanted to hold off on the coup until it was clear how the election results would turn out. If the results were for the NSP, they may not have proceeded with the coup."

"But the Cubans, who were the driving military force of the coup, would not call it off," Lightchurch added. "They may have instead decided on accelerating the plan. So they started the coup even before the election results were in. They didn't want to lose their chance at a second invasion of Grenada."

Wilson stopped pacing and sat down. "The Chinese then got cold feet, so they stopped distribution of the heavy weapons and called off their involvement. They hung the Cubans out to dry."

Madeline now began pacing. "But they couldn't be found with all this heavy gear, so they had to hide it or get rid of it." She stopped in her tracks. "But where?"

They all sat around scratching their heads. Wilson wondered to himself, *Where do you hide so much stuff?*

"They can't take it back to the Wong site. That's for certain," Lightchurch said.

"You know, it bothered me that we didn't have time to check out the whole Wong site last night," Madeline said. "Suppose the gear was there on-site, and we just didn't see it while we were there. We never drove to the west side of the construction site where there are other buildings."

"You're right, Maddie. Suppose it never left the site." Wilson jumped to his feet again. "Suppose they had it there and decided it was a no go? Then they hid the weapons by putting them back into containers."

"The next step would be getting the containers where they could not be found," Lightchurch said. "How would they do that?"

"Place them on a ship during all this chaos caused by the coup. No one has been watching the harbor." Wilson looked from person to person as he spoke. "And there's a Chinese ship in port as we speak, loading containers on board."

"You mean the *Shanghai Maiden?*"

"Yes. As far as I know, they may have been loading that ship all night." Wilson looked at his watch. "We have to hurry." He pulled out his handgun and checked his magazine. "Maddie— you're with me."

***

He and Madeline ran to the door, threw it open, and jumped into the pickup truck. He drove like a madman out onto the street and turned toward the Springs Main Road. They encountered an accident at the supermarket that had backed up traffic. Wilson turned onto a back street and, after some confusion, soon came to a road Madeline recognized that would take them down to the marina. After a few minutes, they encountered water-laden streets again and turned onto Lagoon Road. That led into central Saint George's, but they were driving slowly due to the flooded conditions.

As they crawled along the road that circumnavigated the marina basin, Madeline kept a lookout for the *Shanghai Maiden*. It was hard to see anything as light rain continued to fall. They could see that the lagoon and marina were packed with many smaller craft that had been moored there for protection from the storm and the threatening waves. They drove all the way around the lagoon to the freight dock where the black freighter would be if it was still loading containers.

They reached the main gate of the dock and found it locked. There was no one on guard. They got out of the truck, ran through the rain around to the fence, and looked at the loading area. No cranes were operating, and only two ships were tied up at the freight terminal.

The *Shanghai Maiden* was not there. Nobody was.

"Now what?" Wilson asked Madeline.

"I don't know. They must have left a while ago because I can't see them in the inner harbor," Madeline said. "We can drive over to the cruise ship terminal and look out on Saint George's Bay, but the streets may be blocked. Or we can head back to Grand Anse. Either way, we won't see very far in this rain."

They sloshed through pools of water to the truck and climbed in, soaked to the bone. They had missed it.

Then there was a break in the rain, and just at the edges of their vision, they saw the black stern of a freighter laden with containers on her deck. It was just leaving the inner harbor for the open bay. Then the rain closed in again.

"Shit! Goddamnit!" Wilson shouted, pounding his fists on the dashboard. "I've been watching this ship every day since I've been here and today it slips away just like that."

"They're making for the open sea. There's no way we can catch them now."

Just then Lightchurch's Rover pulled up alongside them in the rain. Wilson stared straight ahead to where the black freighter had last been seen. Madeline climbed out of the truck and ran to the rear window of the Land Rover. She reported what they had witnessed.

"I'll call the chief and see if there's anything he can do." Lightchurch rolled up his window and began dialing. Madeline crawled back in the truck to get out of the rain and waited with Wilson for news.

After five minutes, Nash rapped on the truck window and beckoned them to Lightchurch's Rover. They stood outside his back window in the drizzle while he spoke. "The chief said there's nothing he can do. The few coast guard patrol boats he has are tied up patrolling the volcano and the airport to make sure none of the Cubans can make a run for it. He said even if he could free one up, it would be too small and lightly armed a craft to stop a full-size freighter." He looked disappointed. "In any case, the *Shanghai Maiden* will be in international waters within a half hour and then we'll have no jurisdiction."

"We're all done then," Wilson said. He looked at Madeline in despair. There was silence for several moments as their failure sank in.

Then Lightchurch spoke. "If you're up for it, the chief said they're stretched thin at the airport and you two could join his men there to help cover the perimeter."

***

At 7:00 p.m., rain was still falling intermittently in the darkness, but the wind was dying down after a late surge of fury right after sunset. Wilson and Madeline were stationed on the north side of the airport near the westernmost service doors of the airport terminal. They had been moved around three times to where they were needed as a supplement to the police cordon that surrounded the main terminal building. They hoped this would be their final deployment as the hostage crisis neared its end.

The entire day had been consumed by conflict, with the twenty-six remaining Cubans holding seventeen hostages—five airport employees and twelve innocent passengers. Fighting all day had killed several additional Cubans and wounded ten more police officers. No hostages had been killed since noon when negotiations with the Cuban commander, Cortez, had been taken over directly by the chief himself.

A grand deal had been arranged for the release of all passengers and two employees if an aircraft was made available to fly the Cubans to Caracas, where the chief had been assured by the Venezuelan government that they would be taken into custody and punished. The Venezuelan government would then repatriate the three hostages back to Grenada. But nobody trusted the Maduro government.

For this purpose, a Caribbean Airlines plane had been made available for the mission. The ATR 72-600, with twin turboprop engines, was a steady workhorse of a plane that could take off and land under the most severe conditions and on short runways. It was an ideal choice for this flight in bad weather. It had been fueled and brought to the far end of the terminal where the Cubans would exit the building with their hostages and walk across the tarmac to a small staircase and up onto the plane.

The hostages who remained behind would be released as the plane began its taxi toward the main runway. That was the plan and also the part of the exchange that worried everyone. Would something go wrong, and would hostages die unprotected on the tarmac?

During the boarding of the plane, Wilson and Madeline would support the policemen by securing the northwest corner of the terminal on the tarmac in case anyone ran away in that direction. It seemed unlikely that one of the Cubans would try to escape just before getting on the plane, but stranger things had happened in these types of situations.

Wilson was still in shock. Tori Vargas's face ran through his subconscious. He couldn't turn off the image of her tortured body jammed into the suitcase. Occasionally, an image of her in her bikini as he remembered their afternoon of fun on the beach was juxtaposed in his memory. The contrast between the pleasant and the dreadful was overwhelming. He found it hard to concentrate on their task, just waiting. He needed some action to take his mind off her death.

Madeline was standing twenty feet away. "Hey, Wilson. You OK?" She kept an eye on him, wary that he was losing it just when they needed to be at their best.

He didn't respond, so she strode over and squared off in front of him, getting in his face. "Come on, Robert." She placed her left hand on his chin to shake his head, gaining his attention. "We're about to load up now. Snap out of it."

He looked in her eyes and saw determination and sympathy. "Yeah. I'm OK."

"You look like shit." She smiled and slapped him lightly on the cheek. "Get with it, man."

Finally, in darkness, the moment for boarding had arrived. The airplane was sitting a hundred feet from the building, the propeller on the far side of the craft turning slowly. The one on the near side—the boarding side—was shut down.

A door opened halfway down the west side of the terminal. A hostage, apparently one of the airport employees based on her outfit of khaki pants and a blue uniform shirt, hands tied behind her back, was pushed into the glare of the exterior terminal lights. She looked terrified. Then another came out, hands also bound. A Cuban followed, pointing an AK-74 at the hostages and dragging another female hostage with him. Nothing happened. Then the whole mob of hostages intermixed with Cubans surged out, and, as a group, they shuffled toward the aircraft. Wilson could almost feel the tension that pervaded all the parties: Cubans, hostages, police, Madeline, and himself.

The assemblage of bodies reached the staircase and began boarding the plane. First three Cubans boarded the plane and secured the flight crew and then several more Cubans climbed on board. A hostage was pushed forward and then another climbed the steps.

There was a scuffle as one of the hostages refused to get on the plane. There was shouting and fighting—and then a gunshot. It was unclear what had happened. A body fell to the ground, and both hostages and captors leaped back in shock, screaming and shoving.

"I won't go wid you!"

Then another shot.

As if on cue, everyone began running to the right and away from the plane. Some of the hostages ran back toward the door they had left from the terminal. The Cuban soldiers cut them down with automatic rifle fire as they ran for safety. A few of the hostages ran toward the corner of the building where Wilson and Madeline stood guard.

Then the airplane seemed to lift off the tarmac, erupting in a huge fireball. Something had gone desperately wrong. There was confusion and panic on the tarmac as pieces of the aircraft flew through the air, some burning. Everyone near the plane ran toward Wilson and Madeline, hostages and Cubans alike. There was much gunfire now, some coming from the terminal as police began picking off Cubans. At the same time, the Cubans returned fire and ran to catch up to the fleeing hostages. Their only chance was surrounding themselves with innocent bodies again and fleeing from the hail of bullets.

Ten frightened people ran directly at Wilson and Madeline, hostages with wild eyes and screaming mouths. Shouting soldiers tried to catch up, shooting as they ran, sometimes at the hostages they chased. Both Wilson and Madeline had their handguns up and began shooting the running people who held guns in their hands. They found it difficult to take a clear shot with everybody mixed together.

Within seconds, the fleeing crowd was on them, all mixed up, as hostages reached the corner of the building. But one Cuban, a tall man with a mustache, caught up with a woman and grabbed her by the neck just as he reached Wilson. He ducked behind her and put a gun to her head.

"You! El Americano," he shouted. "I will kill you now."

He pointed his gun at Wilson just as the woman twisted in his grip. He fired at the same moment that Wilson did. All three people, Wilson, Cortez, and the woman, fell to the ground. The woman screamed and wrestled herself free. She crawled away from Cortez, who had landed in a sitting position on the ground. He swung his gun around and shot again, just as Wilson fired from the ground. They both fell backward and stopped moving.

Madeline ran up and shot Cortez in the head as he lay there, possibly trying for another shot, or in the throes of death. Wilson did not move. Madeline dropped to the ground next to him and searched for a pulse as black-booted police ran past her after the last living Cuban.

No pulse. "Help! I need help here!" She began applying CPR on Wilson. She pumped his chest even as she shouted again for help. "Start breathing, damn you!" She tried to focus in spite of a surge of emotion and adrenaline. "Breathe, Robert. Breathe."

A paramedic ran up and took over the care of the fallen man. He checked for a pulse and stopped CPR. He checked Wilson's eyes for reaction.

Madeline sat back on the tarmac and cried openly. "Has it all come to this?" she murmured as Wilson's body lay there on the tarmac and rain fell from the heavens on everyone.

Chapter 20

Thursday

"I must join the PM and the chief in an hour to develop a joint statement for the governor general," Lightchurch said. "We must also create a record of everything that has happened here over the last few weeks. Perhaps there are lessons to be learned."

"We're ready to proceed, Sir," Madeline said. "But it will take weeks to sort everything out."

"How are you faring today, Robert?" His eyes drifted over to Wilson, who sat in a chair at the table. "Have you recovered enough to carry on?" Lightchurch was concerned about Wilson's near-death experience.

"I'll be all right, Sir. My ribs are a bit rough, but I'll make it." Wilson ran his fingers over his heart, where the bullet had smashed into the vest he was wearing. "Lucky, I guess."

"I was shot once while wearing a bulletproof vest in Indonesia. Knocked the piss and vinegar right out of me." Lightchurch chuckled. "Ribs were sore for I don't know how long."

Madeline gave Wilson a severe look. "Lucky I made you put a vest on."

He winced and gave her a thumbs-up.

They all chuckled at his reaction. Morgan, Nash, and Mitchell were there as well for the after-action meeting. Luckily, none of the team had been seriously injured during the coup.

"After it was all cleared up last night, the chief has ninety-four wounded or captured insurgents, Cubans and Venezuelans." Lightchurch read from a list in his hand. "There were eighty-seven insurgents killed as well as at least thirty-seven of his police officers. They're still counting up the number of wounded policemen."

"A lot of hostages were killed by those bastards," Nash said. "But what happened to the plane?"

"We just don't know yet what happened on board the plane," Madeline said. "There was an initial explosion on the plane that somehow lit up one of the fuel tanks. The forensic people and the Eastern Caribbean Civil Aviation Authority have already begun an investigation. It may be months before we know for certain."

"You know, Tori Vargas gave us the key to unravel this coup before she died," Wilson said. "She suffered a terrible death because she helped us."

"Cortez punished her, all right," Madeline said. "I wish there was something we could have done to protect her, but everything happened so quickly."

"I'll ask Langley if we can locate her parents. Maybe help them out in some way. We owe her that." Wilson looked at the floor, and no one spoke for a full minute.

After a thoughtful silence, Lightchurch turned to Wilson. "Robert, how were the Russians involved in all this?"

Wilson breathed deeply and then winced as his ribs warned him not to disturb them. "I'm not sure they were directly involved in the coup. We suspect they played a role in creating unrest during the elections by doing what they do best—interfering with social media and creating dissent. But in the coup itself, nothing."

Madeline then asked, "But what were they doing with all that diving activity?"

Wilson said, somewhat cautiously. "It appears—and this has not been confirmed yet—that they were playing their own game of tapping into an important undersea communications cable. The Southern Caribbean Fiber Cable runs right in the area where they were diving for several days. We know they went under with specialized equipment that may have been used to splice into the cable so that they'd have an independent tap into it."

"A lot of sensitive information runs through that channel," Lightchurch said. "It would be useful for them to listen in to the plans for and commerce of all the islands. And they're experts at that sort of thing."

"It could also be used for the introduction of misinformation or viruses into the system. I'm preparing an investigation into exactly what they were doing through a local contractor here in Grenada," Wilson said. "More on that later."

"And the Shanghai Maiden?"

"This morning I asked that a satellite be tasked to track the *Shanghai Maiden* to see where she went," Wilson said. "I just received an initial track for her as of this morning when the weather cleared. Here's an image of her sailing southwest toward Venezuela. She's only two hundred eighty miles from here."

"But she left by ten in the morning," Morgan said. "She should be four or five hundred miles away at normal speed."

"Look at this satellite photo." Wilson spun his laptop around so that they could all see the photo. The picture showed a large patch of sea with a freighter in the center. The scale was such that they could clearly see the ship's deck, which was covered with stacks of sea containers."

"These are the containers she had on her when she left port?" Lightchurch asked.

"Apparently," Wilson said.

"At least the weapons are off the island," Maddie commented.

Everyone in the room was silent. They didn't have an answer to that question.

Lightchurch stood up. "Well, I must drive over to the PM's office for the meeting. Call me in the next few minutes if you come up with any good news."

"There is one bright spot, Sir," Nash said. "The earthquakes have stopped for now. They say we won't have any big eruption today."

Madeline smiled. "And Radio Free Grenada is back on the air playing soca and calypso music."

On that note, with a grim smile on his face, Lightchurch left the warehouse. The others dispersed to their duties or drove home for some rest after the last few harrowing days.

Wilson and Madeline drove to the Hempstead for a celebratory rum punch. Gordon was tending the main bar and worked his way over to talk.

"Mr. Wilson, have you heard the news? They might raise the volcano alert to level red tomorrow. My source said it getting mighty hot and lots of lava been flowing under the sea." He grinned as he waved his arms, suggesting a big explosion. "Whole island could go up in smoke. Boom!"

"No, Gordon," Wilson said. "It's news to me. Seems like lots of things have been getting hot around here."

"Yes. Well, Radio Free Grenada got the inside scoop on dis, so it mus' be true. You know they predicted the election results too. They pretty good at this stuff." Gordon moved down the bar and tended to another customer.

"Is he always so excitable?" Madeline asked.

"Sometimes, Maddie." Wilson smiled. "But he's got the inside scoop on all sorts of things." They both laughed and sipped their drinks.

They sat in silence and listened to the recorded music that played over the bar's Stingray system. Khalid's song "Young

Dumb & Broke" came on, and Gordon and two other workers behind the bar sang along.

"I better check out of the hotel and find a new place if I'm staying here two or three extra weeks to wrap this up," Wilson said. "I can't stay at the Hempstead after all that has happened."

"You'll never find a room. They're all booked up," Madeline said, a sly smile on her face. She pulled her barstool next to his. "You could stay at my flat if you want. But I don't have a couch."

She leaned over and kissed Wilson on the cheek.

Wilson smiled weakly. "I don't know. It may not be a good idea."

"We can take it slow while you recover your energy," she whispered.

"That sounds like an offer I can't refuse." He reached out and put an arm around her shoulder as she snaked her arm around his waist.

He looked sideways at her and smiled. "Does that mean we may do something unprofessional tonight?"

She chuckled. "Perhaps."

About the Author

Fred G. Baker is a hydrologist, historian, and writer living in Colorado. He is the author of *An Imperfect Crime, Desert Sanctuary, Zona: The Forbidden Land, The Black Freighter,* and the *Modern Pirate Series* of short and long stories. He is also the author of nonfiction works such as *Growing Up Wisconsin, The Life and Times of Con James Baker of Des Moines, Chicago, and Wisconsin, The Light from a Thousand Campfires* (with Hannah Pavlik), and others.

***

Request for Reviews.

Thank you for reading my book. If you enjoyed it, please write a review on Amazon.com. Reviews are important to help authors get the word out on their books. I would appreciate your time to write one.

Please look for my other books on Amazon and Kindle Books. Just type in my name to see other titles that may be of interest to you. You can also check out my website at www.othervoicespress.com.